TEMPLEMAN, R.
.....

Sherlock Holmes &
.....

| 6/04 | KENILWORTH COMMUNITY | | 2 2 JUN 2010 |
|------|---------------------|---|-----------|
| PVI | AJ webb SERVICES KM | | |
| 53k | | | |
| St Michaels | | | |
| Arden | castel troma | | |
| Charles | Murray. R. | | |
| Philpov | Etter | | |
| Clarke | Culworth | | |
| Buck | Carpenter | | |
| | | | |

This item is to be returned on or before the latest date above.
It may be borrowed for a further period if not in demand .

**Warwickshire**
County Council

**Libraries · Heritage · Trading Standards**

# SHERLOCK HOLMES AND THE CHINESE JUNK AFFAIR
## and other stories

Here are three short stories, each involving Sherlock Holmes and Dr Watson. In THE CHINESE JUNK AFFAIR they are in a desperate search to find the truth about an invention which could endanger Britain and the Empire. THE TICK TOCK MAN sees them on a walking holiday in Derbyshire, where their tranquillity is shattered by a curious death and a talking raven. Finally, in THE TROPHY ROOM, they are presented with a classic locked room mystery.

ROY TEMPLEMAN

# Sherlock Holmes and The Chinese Junk Affair

## And Other Stories

*Complete and Unabridged*

LINFORD
*Leicester*

First published in Great Britain in 1998 by
Breese Books Limited
London

First Linford Edition
published 1999
by arrangement with
Breese Books Limited
London

British Library CIP Data

Templeman, Roy
    Sherlock Holmes and The Chinese junk affair
    & other stories.—Large print ed.—
    Linford mystery library
    1. Holmes, Sherlock (Fictitious character)
    —Fiction
    2. Detective and mystery stories, English
    3. Large type books
    I. Title
    823.9'14 [F]

    ISBN 0–7089–5603–3

Published by
F. A. Thorpe (Publishing) Ltd.
Anstey, Leicestershire

Set by Words & Graphics Ltd.
Anstey, Leicestershire
Printed and bound in Great Britain by
T. J. International Ltd., Padstow, Cornwall

This book is printed on acid-free paper

# Contents

# Contents

# Sherlock Holmes and the Chinese Junk Affair

I wrote a full account of what I chose to call 'The case of the Chinese junk' as soon as Holmes had brought it to a successful conclusion. He insisted however that, like official government papers, it should not be published for at least thirty years. 'By that time you and I will no doubt have passed on, my dear Watson.'

The reason why Holmes wished it to be kept secret was because it involved national security and the highest persons in the land. To have let the facts of the case be known to certain powerful nations abroad would have done Britain little good and given comfort to our possible enemies.

The case began in a typical London fog which swirled around and in which ghostly apparitions came and went. It was welcomed only by the undertakers who always became busy as the elderly with chest problems gasped and coughed their last in an effort to breathe.

Holmes and I had been out on a visit to a mutual friend who was in a bad way and wished us to witness his will. Holmes picked up a card which had been pushed under the door in our absence. He unbuttoned his coat with one hand, and held the card with the other, turned it over, and put it on the mantelshelf. We hung our coats and hats on the clothes stand and prepared to settle down before the comfort of the fire before partaking of the supper Mrs Hudson had left on a napkin-covered tray.

Holmes nodded his head towards the card on the mantelshelf. 'Mycroft wishes to see us in his office at ten o'clock sharp tomorrow. 'Of utmost national importance,' he writes. Sounds interesting, Watson.'

'Let us hope it takes us out of London, away from this fog. I must confess, Holmes, I find this particular fog most depressing and unpleasant. But what can you expect with thousands of people like ourselves sitting in front of blazing fires and at the same time fouling the outside air with thick black smoke. Ugh! If only a decent wind would come and blow it away.'

We ate in silence. I could tell Holmes was thinking about the summons from his brother Mycroft. 'Of utmost national importance'. Like Holmes I pondered on the words, for I knew that Mycroft was not a person to use a phrase like 'Utmost national importance', without due cause. Holmes was now relaxed in his easy chair, legs outstretched and eyes closed. What game was afoot, what would tomorrow bring? His reclining frame would then be fully alert, his brilliant reasoning mind selecting priorities of action and then, like a dog following a scent, tenacious until it was solved. His extreme languor now was the complete opposite to the driving energy I was to witness in the days ahead.

\* \* \*

Giving ourselves plenty of time to reach Whitehall because the fog, although thinned considerably, still made the traffic much slower than usual, we set out next morning. We arrived at Mycroft's office as the clock struck ten o'clock. He greeted us warmly, but after we were seated his manner changed. His face became serious, his voice matching in sombre tone. 'Sherlock, the matter is serious. So serious, I am to take you both to be briefed by the Prime Minister and a Cabinet minister right away.'

By Jove, I thought, looking at Mycroft and listening to his conversation, I could see why the Prime Minister placed such reliance upon Mycroft's judgement and discretion.

Mycroft was seven years older than Sherlock, both brothers possessing exceptional powers of observation and deduction. Mycroft was the civil servant who, using his great brain, was able to give overall advice upon how any particular event would affect not only one branch of government, but the whole; foreign trade and diplomatic implications too.

His ability to absorb and pigeon-hole information, combined with instant recall made this possible. He lodged in Pall Mall and his club was the Diogenes. According to Holmes, Mycroft *was* Whitehall. I do not think this was any exaggeration. He was the undisputed expert.

I could not help but contrast Holmes's slim tall figure and hawk-like appearance with that of Mycroft's. Although having the same look of alertness as Holmes, his body was heavily built, almost gross, his movements slow. Exercise was foreign to him, food I imagine his vice. Yet despite his unwieldy body, one could not be but impressed by his noble brow, his deep-set eyes and most of all his great presence.

A four-wheeler was already standing by and the short journey to 10 Downing Street was soon accomplished. Mycroft then returned to his office.

We were ushered into the sanctuary of the Prime Minister. It seemed that nothing had changed since last we were here. Lord Bellinger, austere, high-nosed, eagle-eyed, dominant as ever, rose from his chair and shook our hands. We sat down on the two chairs facing his desk, whilst he and Sir Simon Clayton sat facing us. The Premier's countenance was gaunt and worried. He leaned forward and spoke to us in a voice full of gloom.

'Mr Holmes, I have asked you and Dr Watson here to discuss a most serious and worrying situation. It could affect the future security of this country.'

He paused. 'I and those members of the Cabinet who are privy to the situation have already sought the opinions and advice from the best scientific brains in industry and our universities, presenting the problem as a hypothetical one of course.' He drummed his fingers on the desk. 'Unfortunately none were able to give us much help. They left us only with masses of data and possibilities. Some considered it was possible, others stated it was a preposterous idea and was too laughable to even contemplate.'

He stood up. 'Now perhaps you would be good enough to retire with Sir Simon, the minister most involved in this matter. Hear from him first hand, the facts.' He looked at Sir Simon, then Holmes. 'And later return to give me your opinion of the case, also whether you will take it on or not?'

Holmes said, 'I will do my best, Prime Minister, and I can assure you that if I and Dr Watson can help in any way after hearing what Sir Simon has to say, we will do so.'

Lord Bellinger nodded. 'We have not forgotten your expertise in solving the Bruce-Partington naval plans case, but I can assure you the loss of those plans, serious as they were at the time, cannot compare with this matter.'

We withdrew to a smaller room nearby and Holmes and I sat on the large comfortable settee, whilst Sir Simon sat opposite in a leather armchair. He helped us to coffee and asked if we had any other urgent calls upon our time that morning, which Holmes assured him we had not. Holmes put down his coffee cup and said, 'Sir Simon, I am aware that this matter is of the utmost importance. I would ask you therefore when relating the facts, to give every detail, no matter how irrelevant it may appear to you. Dr Watson and I are in no hurry, so do not feel in any way obliged to consider our time. Please take as long as you wish, but do include all the facts. The first telling of any case is the most important.'

Sir Simon put his coffee cup down upon the tray by his chair. 'I am much indebted to you and will try to remember every fact, no matter how irrelevant it may appear to me. But I fear it will be a long account.'

Holmes nodded, 'No matter, no matter.'

Sir Simon began. 'I met Rodger Hardy by accident last September. I thought at the time it was accidental, later I realised it was a well planned meeting on his part. Rodger Hardy was a contemporary of mine from university days. He was clever, had a brilliant brain. His parents had met a tragic end whilst on holiday and his uncle had put him through university. The family were industrialists and had a flair for invention. There are many things in use every day which they either had invented or had a hand in developing. However, due to neglecting patenting rights and pouring money into developing an invention which other companies, and the State I might add, were to benefit from, the family went bankrupt.

'The uncle became a recluse in the family home, Halam Hall. It became a ruin, part of it almost falling down. The surrounding farms and land were gradually sold off, until only the Hall and a few acres of wooded land the Hall stood on, remained.

'Rodger meanwhile had gone abroad, it was rumoured to China, and nothing was seen of him for years, save that I would occasionally hear he had been seen in London, on what must have been rare visits to this country.

'So it was a pleasure and a surprise when I met him again. We had much to talk over, old times, old friends, you know the sort of thing one discusses with a friend after so many years' absence. We were almost ready to part company because I had an appointment to keep, when he said 'Look here, Simon, can't we meet again, have a meal? Besides, I want to show you something.' I was puzzled by the last remark. He went on, 'Look, there is a very good train service that stops at my local station at ten past six. I could meet you with the dogcart and we could have dinner together, you staying overnight.'

'And so I accepted his invitation, both because I liked Rodger and was intrigued as to what he had to show me. I was widowed two years ago and I find myself with a lot of time on my hands at weekends. Of course, I am invited by friends still, but it is not the same without my wife — a little embarrassing really for them, and awkward, I find, for myself. Invitations to parties, functions and meetings, well that is different. So you see I looked forward to the visit; he being a bachelor, there was a sort of common ground between us.

'I arrived at his little local station the following weekend, and there was Rodger waiting with the dogcart.'

Holmes interrupted, 'This was late September I gather?'

'Yes, the evenings were drawing in but the countryside was a joy to see.

10

I enjoyed the leisurely ride along the country lanes, smelling the late flowering honeysuckle in the hedgerows. I am a countryman at heart, you know, was brought up in it and have never lost the love for it; the woods, fields and the wild creatures that hide there.

'I always felt at ease with Rodger. He has a wonderful sense of humour and hundreds of stories about the happenings in his part of the world we, in Europe, hardly know exists.

'We turned in off the lane between two tall stone pillars. The state of Halam Hall could be guessed at by the untidy sight of grass growing against the rusty iron gates. They had never been closed for years. The winding driveway lined with rhododendron bushes was overgrown with weeds and grass. Overhead the rooks in the trees cawed as we arrived at the turning circle of the Hall.

'The Hall was large, much larger than one would expect a Hall to be. But on a closer look it was clear that over the years there had been many alterations and additions. Fashion and individual

11

whims were evident, culminating in an unbalanced architectural mongrel of a place. It was made worse by the state of disrepair. Long neglect over many years and ivy allowed to run rampant into the roof had caused much damage. Part of the rear extension had begun to fall in. The whole place gave an air of neglect and decay.

'A boy came running down the steps from his quarters over the stables to take the horse. I remember he was a ginger-haired lad and I could see, by the grin on his face, and the way he touched his cap to Rodger, that he worshipped him. The same pleasure in serving Rodger was evident in the few servants who worked part time at the Hall. Mrs Penrose, the cook, and her daughter came every day from the village. An elderly retired gardener and the ginger-haired boy attempted to keep the jungle of weeds from swamping the grounds. To them Rodger was still lord of the manor and they gave him that respect.

'Before dinner, Rodger showed me over the grounds and it took me back to the years when he and I went to the home of a fellow student and that was in a similar state. I wondered if Rodger remembered that occasion and considered, as did I, that it was a little ironic.

'We returned to the main entrance of the Hall and I made a reference to the remark he had made to me when we had first renewed our acquaintance that, 'He had something to show me'.

' 'Oh, yes!' he replied, 'but after dinner would be best.'

'Inside the Hall it was dark and dingy and as one looked about it, one could see from the lack of furniture that many, no doubt fine, pieces had been sold by his uncle. Likewise when I looked at the walls, there were many places showing light patches where paintings and pictures had once hung.

'The dining-room though was welcoming and comfortably furnished. In the grate, logs burned and crackled, giving a much appreciated warmth after our walk around the grounds in the rather chill evening air.

13

'Rodger Hardy had thrown away any form of usual convention by combining the purposes of the dining-room and drawing-room into one. A dining-table and chairs were close to the window, which looked out over the uncut lawns, whilst three large leather-covered chairs, and an even larger sofa, were grouped close around the hearth to constitute the drawing-room.

'Rodger grinned and asked me to excuse his rather bohemian way of life, 'I'm a bachelor and living in all parts of the world I find comfort is the essential thing'. Although he had made enough money abroad to have renovated the Hall easily, it was not his intention to do so. 'I intend to eventually put it on the market, so that is why the Hall is in such a poor state'. Which he later did of course.

'The two of us ate an excellent meal cooked by Mrs Penrose and served by her daughter. They had stayed on late to do so. It was nearly two hours on when Rodger referred to that which he wished to show me. 'My great grandfather made a fortune you know from the railways; not building them, but from the locomotive engineering side. To cut a long story short, my great grandmother decided she would like a ballroom built, but because great grandfather considered it would spoil even further the outline of the Hall, he decided to excavate and build it underground. This he did. The Duke of Portland I understand did likewise, and I am informed the eccentric Fifth Duke spent millions of pounds building a splendid underground one. They say it was the largest underground ballroom in Europe, without supporting pillars. Also, he built miles of underground roadways under his estate at Welbeck Abbey in Nottinghamshire. Can you imagine it? The roadways were lit by gas lamps and he had instructions given that his workers should never abase themselves or acknowledge his presence, but treat him as though he were a tree. He was truly a very eccentric person.

' 'One of these underground roads even extended nearly as far as the local railway station, to where he would travel in his coach. On emerging into the daylight, he would draw the blinds so no one would observe him. On arriving he entrained, and down to London he would go.'

'I remembered the Duke because he was involved in a court case, and mentioned this to Rodger.

' 'Yes, that is correct. After the Duke's death in 1879, in a most celebrated case at the time, a man named Druce claimed to be the legitimate son of the Duke, he being the son of a secret marriage between the Duke and a woman of low birth by the name of Druce, who ran a bazaar in Baker Street. Forgive me, Simon, I digress. Follow me and I will show you the ballroom.'

'We went out of the dining-room into the entrance hall where, to the left, was a very wide door. Rodger opened it. 'Here is the entrance, and the steps down to the ballroom. You will notice the ballroom was never finished. Great grandmother broke her hip and, because she could no longer dance, lost interest in the ballroom idea and so it has remained, just an underground concrete shell.' '

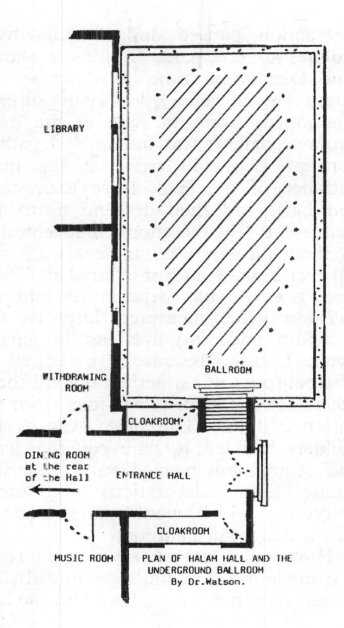

LIBRARY

BALLROOM

WITHDRAWING
ROOM

CLOAKROOM

DINING ROOM
at the rear
of the Hall

ENTRANCE HALL

CLOAKROOM

MUSIC ROOM

PLAN OF HALAM HALL AND THE
UNDERGROUND BALLROOM
By Dr.Watson.

Sir Simon paused and, looking from Holmes to me, said, 'I think I should now take some time to describe this room. The entrance led as I have already mentioned, from the side of the main entrance hall. It was intended, I gather, that guests would arrive at the main entrance of the Hall, leave their coats and hats, and then descend down the staircase to the ballroom. The entrance to the ballroom was six feet wide and ten feet high. I later measured it. There were twenty wide steps down into the ballroom which measured thirty-five feet in width and sixty-five feet in length. Again I know because I measured it. The ballroom was a perfect oblong shape except for the protruding stairs from the entrance doors. The place was as the builders had left it, bare concrete walls and ceiling, but needed only plastering, ornate ceiling, decorations; you know, everything which would have made it into a delightful ballroom.

'However, it was what was in the room that made me stop and stare in disbelief. Along the centre of the floor was the keel of a boat. Beginning a few feet from the bottom of the staircase and ending a few feet from the rear wall. Over fifty feet in length. I could see it was to be a boat, because the ribs down one side were already in place.

'If that was not enough of a shock, to see a boat being built underground with no hope of ever getting it out, then it was compounded by the sight of ten grinning Chinamen standing in a row, who, when I stared at them, each in turn bowed from the waist and continued to grin. Mr Holmes, I thought it about as bizarre a situation as one could ever come across.'

I looked sideways at Holmes and saw the look of supreme pleasure upon his face. An architect who is asked to design a cathedral or an artist commanded to paint the Royal Monarch could not have had a more satisfying expression.

Here was not a lurid domestic murder or a criminal case of burglary which seemed to have been Holmes's lot for some time now, but a case that had all the trappings of mystery and intrigue, to equal the best of his others. It involved the highest in the land and the story that was already unique was only yet half told.

'I think I had better ring for some more coffee. I'm afraid I have much more to tell,' said Sir Simon. Holmes eased himself in his chair to make himself more comfortable.

'I have listened to many strange accounts in my life but I am sure Dr Watson will agree that this looks like being the strangest yet.'

I agreed and took the opportunity to also stretch out my legs. The coffee was brought in almost at once and after Sir Simon did the honours, continued with his account.

'I turned to Rodger and saw he was smiling. He said, 'Let us retire and have a drink by the fire and let these good chaps rest after their day's labour.' He waved his hand to them and they in turn, grinned and bowed to us again.

'Over drinks Rodger explained that the Chinese were constructing a full-sized ocean-going wooden junk, and that it would take about six months to build. He wanted me to visit Halam Hall and observe the progress, month by month.

'When I laughed and asked why he was building a Chinese junk, in a building where there was no hope of ever getting it out, he only smiled and replied, 'Well, if you will come down once a month and observe its construction, eventually on completion, all will be revealed.' I ask you, Mr Holmes, what man could resist such an invitation?

'Each month I journeyed to Halam Hall and enjoyed an excellent meal, good wine and a complete rest from the London scene. I looked forward to those weekends. Rodger was wonderful company. He had such a huge store of anecdotes about his years abroad, and his general knowledge of most subjects, like your own, Mr Holmes, is phenomenal; he was a great raconteur and also a good listener.

'Each time I visited, I was shown the progress the Chinamen were making with the construction of the junk. I was surprised and amazed at the amount of timber being used. The progress was quite remarkable.

'On my second visit, for instance, the ribs of the vessel had been completed and the shape and size it would eventually be, was very evident. On my third visit planking was being fastened to the ribs, and on each occasion, the Chinamen ceased work, lined up at the side of the vessel, bowed to me and grinned.'

Holmes interrupted. 'You examined the work then, at close hand?'

'Oh, yes, the carcase of the vessel was constructed of the most substantial timbers. The keel itself of oak must have weighed many tons.

'As the months passed by, I would take a look at the progress they were making from the steps; the Chinamen sawing and planing away. I would wave to the grinning Chinamen upon leaving, looking forward to Rodger's excellent dinner and his company.'

'One other question,' said Holmes. 'Did Rodger Hardy ever give a reason why he had gone to China in the first instance?'

Sir Simon placed his hands together, fingertip to fingertip, as Holmes is prone to do. 'Strange you should ask that, because I, too, was curious. It appeared that he had met at a social gathering Aurel Stein, the Jewish intellectual who had become the Registrar of the Punjab University and Principal of the Oriental College in Lahore.

'Aurel Stein was infatuated with the East and began his archaeological work in the Middle East and then on to Kashmir. But it was his enthusiasm for the wilderness of Central China and the lost cities of the Silk Road that fired the imagination of Rodger Hardy. Aurel Stein talked of the Lop Desert and Mongolia; of the prospects a white man could expect from trading in China. But it was the rumour which Aurel Stein had heard from many sources, that great scientific strides were being made by a number of Chinese scientists in the field of electricity, which excited Rodger.

'The rumour was to do with the passage of electricity without using wire or cable, that was the attraction for him.

He told me it became an obsession to find these scientists, to discover if it were true. He knew that such a discovery would make him a fortune here in Europe and America.

'Bribery and political manoeuvring made it possible for him to travel about in China and search for this small group of scientists, which he of course eventually found and joined. Together they developed what he called the 'Transposer'.'

Holmes repeated the word, 'The 'Transposer', what is that?'

Sir Simon replied, 'I will explain later as I reveal the case. I am sorry, gentlemen, the story is a long one, but please bear with me a while longer.'

Holmes said, 'I find your account fascinating, as I am sure Dr Watson does. Pray proceed.'

Sir Simon leaned forward, his hands placed flat upon his knees. 'It was on my last visit in April when I was to experience the shock of my life, and to have revealed to me the reason why I had been chosen to witness, month by month, the most extraordinary construction of this vessel in the underground ballroom.

'I had been chosen, I realise now, as a reliable witness to observe an invention which could alter the whole balance of power in the world. I can assure you, Great Britain and her Empire could be at great peril from it.'

He paused and his voice became almost conspiratorial. 'I shall never forget that weekend, Mr Holmes. When I visited the ballroom, the vessel was completed; painted with even the masts and sails lain along its deck ready for stepping. The Chinamen, though, were nowhere to be seen. However, surrounding the vessel were ten feet tall wooden posts, at a distance apart of five or six feet. Fastened to the posts starting at the base, and at every foot in height, were strands of copper wire. The whole vessel was caged in with these strands of copper wire, stretching all the way around it.

'There was a buzzing sound too, and Rodger warned me not to touch the wires or put my hand between them as the vessel was being electrically energised.

25

'I walked around the vessel in an almost bewildered state. What was it all about, I asked myself? To say I was perplexed would be putting it mildly. Was Rodger mad? Was *I* mad? I continued to walk around it in silence; my mind puzzled by the whole situation.

'I followed Rodger up the steps and stopped; looked down on the extraordinary scene and, in the entrance hall, for the first time noticed the open door of what was the old cloakroom. I glanced inside and was amazed to see a sort of switchboard with all sorts of dials and switches on it. There were thick electric cables running across the floor, and I could hear the sound of what I presume were powerful generators, also the hiss of a steam engine, used to power the generators.

'When I caught up with Rodger he turned and said, 'I know you are surprised; you want to know what is going on, but I assure you, all will be made clear shortly.'

'I was so surprised, I opened my mouth, but no words came forth. Rodger slapped me on the back. 'Come on, old friend, let us eat, drink and forget all about what you have just seen until — ' He looked at his watch. 'It is ten minutes past seven now. If all goes well, in two hours' time, all will be revealed and I will answer any questions you may care to ask.'

'With that I followed Rodger into the dining-room and after the superb game pie and wines, I soon began to forget the shock I had experienced, and even began to look forward to having the mystery of the goings-on in the ballroom revealed.

'Little did I realise, Mr Holmes, what I was to witness would soon cause me, and the government, the most monumental worry I have ever known. The shift of world power could be in the balance and the way of life altered for everyone.'

Sir Simon rose and poured himself a drink, indicating to Holmes and me that we were welcome to the same if we so wished. Holmes and I shook our heads; we waited with bated breath for Sir Simon to continue, which he did after sitting down.

'I well remember the aged grandfather clock in the dining-room striking the hour of nine. Rodger rose and, excusing himself, said he would be absent for a couple of minutes. It was five past the hour when he returned; he stood by the fireplace and looked down at me.

' 'Well, Simon, I told you that if all goes well in two hours' time all would be revealed, the mystery would be no more, and you will know what it is all about. Now is the time; if you will be so good as to follow me, please.'

'I followed Rodger out of the dining-room, into the hallway and down the ballroom steps. I looked and stood absolutely still. ·I could not believe what I was seeing. I continued to look. Rodger stood behind me and never said a word. There was not a sound to be heard; silence prevailed.

'The electric humming from the generators had stopped, so had the hiss of the steam engine. It was as quiet as the grave. I continued to be speechless, rubbing my eyes as though it might help to explain what I was seeing, or, to put it more accurately, not seeing.'

Sir Simon's voice dropped to almost a whisper. Holmes and I leaned forward to enable us to catch whatever he was to say.

'Mr Holmes, the ballroom was empty! Yes, empty! The electric lights around the room lit up that huge empty space.'

He paused; the seconds ticked by, then he continued in that still muted voice. 'The only things remaining were the wooden poles supporting the lengths of copper wire; still in place, forming a cage, but the vessel itself had vanished into thin air.

'That huge Chinese junk, which only two hours before had taken up the whole space of the ballroom, was gone. I stood there, speechless, as though dumb. Perhaps a minute passed, it may have been more, I don't really remember. My brain could not take it in. That huge vessel weighing thirty, perhaps forty, tons had vanished.

'It would have taken a week at least, I imagine, to have reduced it to scrap, to enable it to have been taken piece by piece, up those steps and out through the doorway. Yet it had vanished, nothing of it remained.

'I felt Rodger's hand upon my shoulder. In a voice we reserve for speaking to someone in a state of shock, as I was, he said, 'Come on, old chap, let's have a drink. I'm sorry I didn't realise it would be such a surprise, well, shock to you.' '

Sir Simon looked at Holmes and then to me. Holmes didn't say anything. I think we were both anxious not to break the spell which the account had created on all three of us. Sir Simon at last continued.

'It was some time before I was back to anything like normality and was able to discuss the phenomenon I had witnessed. Believe me, Mr Holmes, it was truly a phenomenon. The gist of the conversation afterwards was this.

'Rodger described it as 'transposing' matter through space by means of converting solids, by electricity, into waves, which could then be converted back again into the original solid state.

This was how he put it in simple terms, to me, a non-scientific person.

'He then went on to explain that for the past fifteen years he had been working with two Chinese scientists on the project. They had suddenly had a breakthrough five years ago, and had been able to transpose solids by the use of electricity, into a form which enabled them to be transferred for a distance of over twenty miles, then re-form as solids again.

'The Chinese scientists, Rodger said, did not seem interested in the potential of it, only in its discovery. They were now researching into the means of extending the process over greater distances.

' 'I left them to their research, I must confess, with much regret,' he said. 'I had a huge respect for them as friends and for their ability. They were wonderful companions and fifteen years is a long time. In Europe, they would have been prize winners, but thousands of miles away in the heart of China, they worked on their research unsung, and their achievements unknown. China

31

is, in distance and attitudes, miles apart from us in the West.'

'He went on to say how he realised the value, and the huge possibilities the discovery held, and so decided to leave China and take the discovery to Europe.

'Which country should he approach, because he realised that should a war develop, the transposing discovery could be used to great advantage. Heavy guns, supplies of all kinds could be 'transposed' at a few hours' notice and placed at the front where the enemy was weakest.

'Although the British government had treated his family badly over the development of a past invention, and had evaded the patent rights which had led to the family's financial downfall, he still held a certain loyalty to the old country.

'In a nutshell, Mr Holmes, he offered the discovery to the British government for the sum of one million pounds; yes, one million pounds. I had been selected, chosen if you like to put it, to witness the discovery because I was a member of the Cabinet and he considered me a one hundred per cent, cast-iron person to be believed. After all, who would have listened to him, had he tried to sell his discovery without proof? But by setting up the elaborate demonstration in the ballroom, the validity of the discovery was proven beyond a shadow of doubt.'

Sir Simon leaned backwards as though the effort of going through the account had left him drained. He looked at his desk for some time as though forgetting we were present.

Holmes coughed, and said, 'So, Sir Simon, about the transposition.'

Sir Simon appeared to shake himself literally, and took up the story again.

'Next morning we had breakfast and the stable boy brought the dogcart to the door and Rodger and I set off at a brisk pace. I remember that wonderful sunny March morning; it was difficult for me to realise I was taking part in a discovery which could change the world.

'I had lain awake many hours during the night, pondering over the potential, both in war and peace, and the effect it would have on all nations.

'Rodger chatted away about the country-side and the things we were observing; the early growth of the leaves on the hawthorn hedges, a hovering hawk and the fine foals on the stud farm nearby. It all seemed so unreal when I thought about events over the last twelve hours.

'We turned down a narrow lane and shortly arrived by the side of the River Thames. We stopped and looked; and there floating on the water not fifty yards away was the Chinese junk. I wonder, gentlemen, if you have any conception of the effect that sight had upon me? I just sat there and stared and continued to stare. I felt it was just not possible, yet I could not disbelieve what my eyes were seeing.

'On her deck were in line the ten Chinamen. As I got down from the dogcart and approached the junk, they bowed and grinned; just as they had always done. The water slapped against her sides, that solid huge junk held against the tide with ropes fore and aft.

'A plank of wood against the hull acted as a gangway. I was taken around to inspect her and was impressed at the amount of work which must have gone into her building during those six months.

'Returning from inspecting the interior of the vessel to the deck, I observed a photographer on the bank taking pictures of the vessel. Rodger had hired him for the sole purpose of providing a photographic record to substantiate my future verbal account of events to the Prime Minister and Cabinet ministers.

'The visit had lasted perhaps half an hour. We said our farewells and descended the gangplank. Amid more bowing and grinning from the Chinamen, in what seemed no time at all, the Chinamen cast off, raised the rattan sails and were soon sailing down to the sea and out of sight. That was the last I ever saw of the junk or the ten Chinamen.'

We seemed to have been listening to Sir Simon for ages and I think he was a little hoarse by now. Holmes sat upright, his hands clasped together.

'Well, Sir Simon, I am sure it is a

most extraordinary experience you have had, and I know Dr Watson will agree with me when I say that you have given us a very good picture of the situation now facing Her Majesty's Government.

'Correct me if I am wrong, but the problem is not that Her Majesty's Government is particularly worried about the one million pounds being asked, considerable though it is, but that the discovery could be sold to any other powerful nation and cause a shift in power which might be disadvantageous to Britain and the Empire.'

'That is correct,' replied Sir Simon.

Holmes continued. 'I am correct also in assuming that having taken advice from the most learned in the land, no definite conclusion has been reached as to whether this discovery is genuine, or to put it bluntly, a huge confidence trick to extract one million pounds from Her Majesty's Government.' Sir Simon nodded. Holmes continued.

'I assume a time limit to take up the offer has been given, after which time he will take the discovery abroad and offer it to a foreign power?' Again Sir Simon nodded agreement.

Holmes put his fingertips together. 'I gather that there is some difficulty about exchanging the million pounds for the plans, otherwise Her Majesty's Government would have risked being the butt of a confidence trick, obtained the plans and built the apparatus to prove its authenticity?'

'Yes,' replied Sir Simon. 'Rodger will not hand over the plans. He insists that he places several duplicates of the plans with certain reliable establishments — banks, solicitors and the like — on the understanding that, in the event of war, they are sent at once to the person addressed to on the envelope. This will be the Prime Minister of the day.

'Out of the many duplicate sets of plans, one envelope is bound to be dispatched within days of the outbreak of hostilities, even if some are overlooked and arrive late or not at all. The holders of the envelopes do not of course realise the value of the contents.'

Holmes asked, 'What is the reason

Rodger gives for this elaborate exchange system?'

Sir Simon replied, 'Rodger is against the discovery being used for commercial gain. He says the railways, canals and road transport carriers would suffer. Thousands of people would be thrown out of work. Women and children would starve. But by using this method he avoids the commercial use of the discovery, whilst making it available in time of crisis such as war, when it would prove invaluable.'

Holmes nodded and remarked, 'This, however, is contrary to the purpose of leaving his colleagues in China; it was to exploit the invention.'

'I agree, but during the long sea voyage he had time to think about it and decided that it would be of little merit or purpose to become the richest man in the world, if he also became the most hated.'

Holmes agreed. 'So the nub of the situation is, should the discovery be genuine, Her Majesty's Government has only Rodger's word that he has not sold it on the same basis to other foreign powers and, in the event of war, Britain would have no advantage over them?'

Sir Simon agreed. He looked tired now and despondent. The worry of the situation once again upsetting him.

Holmes stroked his chin, stretched himself and said, 'So I and Dr Watson are to do what the learned men refuse to do, state categorically that it is either a huge confidence trick, or a world-shattering discovery which could topple Empires?'

Sir Simon sat upright, as though to show he was again alert and ready to meet Holmes on his own terms. 'That is exactly correct, Mr Holmes. The Prime Minister, the Cabinet members privy to this matter, and your brother Mycroft, concluded that if any person could answer that question, it is undoubtedly yourself.'

He was silent for a few moments. 'Frankly I have no doubts that it is genuine. No power on earth, except that explained by Rodger Hardy to me that weekend, would have been able to have achieved what I saw happen. We look upon you as our only hope in finding out the truth. Will you take it on?'

'You put a lot of onus on our shoulders, do they not, Dr Watson? But we shall do what we can.' Sir Simon ushered us out and a few minutes later we met with the Prime Minister again.

The Prime Minister's eyes held those of Holmes. I felt he was looking both for acceptance of the case by Holmes and also, perhaps, some sign of hope that it might be resolved. I glanced at Holmes and felt as he spoke to the Prime Minister that he seemed, for once, to have reservations about this particular case.

However, he accepted it and promised to pursue it with the utmost vigour, but I now detected a distinct lacking of his usual joy and pleasure at solving what always seemed the unsolvable. It was a great responsibility they had thrust upon his shoulders, and Holmes was well aware of it.

★ ★ ★

For the rest of the day Holmes sat by the fire at 221B Baker Street, referring to scientific books and lapsing into long periods of thinking. I didn't speak to him, not wishing to disturb his train of thought, but got on with my letter writing and pottering about.

I looked out of the window. The unusual Spring fog was clearing and within an hour the sun was beginning to break through.

'You realise, Watson,' said Holmes, at last breaking his long silence, 'that if we accept the fact that the Chinese junk did indeed transpose through the air within the space of two hours, then we must accept this electrical 'transposition' explanation. No other power on earth by the laws of physics as we know them today is capable of achieving this. You can see from the photographs taken that day of the junk on the Thames, that she is large, heavy, and built to be almost indestructible except in the worst typhoon.

'Now, we are told that Rodger Hardy is now visiting America and that he has

41

put Halam Hall up for sale. So, Watson, let us go property hunting.'

I looked up the trains in our Bradshaw and saw we would be better catching the early morning workman's train next day, than setting off now and, on arriving, spend most of our time perhaps searching for overnight accommodation.

Holmes agreed and continued to expound his thoughts to me. 'You see, Watson, we must not lose sight of our brief which is of course to investigate and prove or disprove the genuineness of this electrical transposing device.

'It does no good and serves no useful purpose by thinking it is just not possible. Who would have thought it possible in the heyday of coach travel, that passengers would rush along in armchair comfort at speeds in excess of eighty miles an hour on the railways. Or that London Bridge could be lit at the touch of a switch, on and off, on and off.'

Holmes reeled off facts as though lecturing a body of students.

'Electric lights were installed and illuminated London Bridge in 1881.

Edison invented the electric light in 1879. So we see solid coal was converted to electricity to produce light.

'Way back in 1831 Michael Faraday, an Englishman, and Joseph Henry, an American, discovered independently how to produce electricity,' Holmes continued his lecture from his great fund of knowledge stored in that noble cranium.

'Before all this, Benjamin Franklin originated the idea of electricity. He flew kites in thunderstorms to capture the electricity from the skies. Later, he stated, electricity flowed from positive to negative, but he was wrong in this, because later other scientists proved that electricity flows in the opposite direction from negative to positive. We know that electric fields exist in the space around a charged body. An electric force acts on the charged bodies that enter the field. Particles with unlike charges attract one another, and those with like charges repel.'

He paused and looked at the ceiling and after a few moments continued.

'This is ordinary knowledge, but reflect

upon the amount of progress three dedicated scientists, building upon what is already known, might achieve. It is no use saying, 'Yes, but this is beyond belief, to actually transform solid matter into a form whereby it moves from one place to another, and re-forms itself, that is too absurd.' But is it?

'Would not many of those learned men of a hundred years ago have thought the same about the electric car which first appeared, as you are aware, on the streets of Europe in 1880? A horseless carriage indeed.'

Holmes placed his fingertips together; it was one of his favourite mannerisms when contemplating matters. He looked at me with a serious face.

'Proving the 'Transposer' is a confidence trick may prove very difficult, Watson, but proving it is authentic . . . ' He shook his head slowly from side to side . . . 'Well-nigh impossible.'

He rose from his chair to open the door for Mrs Hudson, bringing in our evening meal.

'Let us enjoy our meal together, for

who knows what tomorrow may bring. We must live in hopes that the gods are kind to us. What say you, Mrs Hudson?'

'I don't know what it is you're referring to, Mr Holmes, but I agree that I hope the gods are kind to us all, tomorrow, and a while after that I hope.'

'Well spoken, Mrs Hudson, and I am sure we shall enjoy our meal, it smells of ambrosia. I see too, you have chilled one of the wines Sir Beconfield gave us last month.'

After the meal and before we settled down for the evening we packed our small cases so as to be ready in the morning to dash out and catch the returning workman's special that would have disgorged its teeming masses on London.

We retired early to bed so as to be fresh and ready for an early start.

'Early to bed, early to rise . . . sleep well, Watson.' Holmes closed his bedroom door quietly.

However, I lay awake some considerable time unable to sleep, going over and over again the incredible story Sir Simon had related to us. The facts defied all logic. A magician makes things disappear only by hiding them away somewhere else. This is what Rodger Hardy had caused to happen, but the means had been scientific. How could Holmes prove it, when it had taken those Chinese scientists years to achieve the means of 'Transposition'.

I could see why the Prime Minister was so concerned. He had indeed placed upon Holmes's shoulders a burden of unbearable magnitude. My old friend could find clues that others missed, even the combined force of Scotland Yard, but even he could not perform miracles. Sleep came to me thankfully at last.

* * *

After rising early and enjoying one of Mrs Hudson's fortifying breakfasts, we took a cab to the station and caught the train with time to spare.

There were a few workers on the train leaving London for jobs outside the capital but, on the whole, the train ran back almost empty.

We had been given the key to Halam Hall before leaving No. 10 by Sir Simon and, so prepared, settled down to admire the countryside as it slid by, a wonderful changing diorama of English history. The backs of terraced houses with vegetable plots soon gave way to larger detached ones with ornamental lawns and larger ones with trees and lakes.

The vista changed to the true countryside, with fields and hedges. What a change from our everyday London scene. At last the train stopped at our destination with hardly any other passengers alighting.

It was a typical Great Western station, the village however sported a 'Station Hotel' where we were able to book a room and leave our cases in the good hands of the rather jovial owner and his buxom wife.

The good man was able to hire us the only horse and trap the village had, and we were soon on our way to Halam Hall.

47

It was a couple of miles out of the village and was exactly as Sir Simon had described it. Shabby, overgrown and even worse now, I suppose, than when he used to visit, having no staff to keep the weeds at bay or mow the lawns. Holmes instructed the driver to return later in the afternoon.

The key turned in the lock easily enough and the huge oak doors swung open. It was at that moment the elderly gardener, who looked after the place and lived in the quarters once occupied by the ginger-haired lad, appeared. He touched his forelock and quickly Holmes explained our intention of wanting to look around the property.

We had taken the precaution of bringing with us two lanterns, and with these lit we set out from the entrance hall to examine the much discussed ballroom.

Firstly though, Holmes requested the elderly caretaker to open up every shutter in every room, so we might later examine the rooms in daylight. Silver changed hands, forelock was once again touched and that worthy man ambled away to do Holmes's bidding.

On descending the stairs, our lanterns lit up that vast empty cavern of a ballroom. Again it was exactly as had been described. Walls, floor and ceiling of bare concrete. All that remained was an electric cable, draped around the walls high up, from which every few yards a light fitting hung. How we wished we could have switched them on. However, by concentrating the lights of both lanterns and examining the walls, floor and ceiling in a systematic way, which took us a considerable time, we examined every foot.

The result was disappointing. We found nothing to give any indication the ballroom had been the site of a most remarkable event. Not a screw, not a nail, not a grain of sawdust remained. Likewise the cloakroom which, we were informed by Sir Simon, had been packed with electrical gear, cables and boards with numerous dials and switches. None of it remained.

We emerged once again into the now

sun-drenched hallway. From there we searched every room, every passage. We removed dustsheets amid clouds of dust, to examine the furniture hidden beneath. We went out into the sunshine to breathe once again fresh air and sneeze the dust from our nostrils.

'Watson, we have searched high and low. I greatly fear we shall not discover any clues here.' Holmes kicked a stone away and continued. 'I fear Rodger Hardy and his team of Chinamen will have gone over every inch to prevent anyone finding out anything.' He reached out with his foot again and kicked another stone away. 'Yet, perhaps that alone gives us our first clue. Why, if the discovery is genuine, should he take such great care to obliterate any sign of the great 'Transposer'?'

I replied, 'Perhaps he just gave the order to his Chinamen to clear away everything, and they took him at his word, being very zealous chaps, and did just that.' Holmes nodded thoughtfully, 'Maybe, maybe.'

We went back into the Hall and looked

again at the downstairs morning-room the Chinamen had used to cook, dine and sleep in. It was obvious from the remaining aroma of oriental spices that this was so. Again outside in the grounds near the overgrown bushes a freshly covered piece of earth indicated where the privy had been sited, and a huge area of burnt grass, covered with charcoal, told us that it was the site where rubbish, shavings and discarded wood had been disposed of. We did though observe a few deep ruts left by the steam tractors near the turning circle at the front of the Hall.

Holmes suddenly turned and, striding back into the Hall, began lighting the two lanterns. 'Watson, we must examine the ballroom again, the answer must be there.'

We spent the next half hour scraping the concrete here and there with an old rusty horseshoe he had picked up in the grounds. The corners and walls we probed with the horseshoe, but proved there was no hidden joint, no secret sliding section, only the rasp of the iron upon the concrete revealing the pebbles, sand and cement beneath years of grime and discoloration.

'Upon my word, Watson, my dear fellow, we have found hardly a single clue to indicate the event ever happened at all, other than the obvious ones, the curry smell, the tractor tracks . . . any dull-witted bobby could not fail to observe these.' He shook his head several times. 'Without clues, I am like a bloodhound without a scent to follow.'

I had never seen Holmes so tired and dejected. I followed him up the steps. Our driver had returned and, following the instructions given us by Sir Simon, we visited the site by the riverside to which the junk had been transposed. But even the hawk-like examination by Holmes revealed nothing more than would have been expected; grass trodden down around the post upon the bank where the junk had been made fast.

'There are so many questions, Watson, I would like the answers to. For instance, assuming it all happened as described by Sir Simon, how did the junk suddenly appear from seemingly nowhere? Did someone in the darkness hear the splash as it arrived? How did the Chinamen know exactly where to find it and make it fast before it floated away?

'One moment I am convinced it is the confidence trick of the century, and the next moment, when I think of the impossibility of moving the junk out of the ballroom and transporting that huge heavy vessel over three miles of countryside, I become more and more convinced of the 'Transposer' discovery.'

I had never seen Holmes so concerned and serious. We returned to the trap and went back to the Hall making sure all was secure and, after again tipping the elderly caretaker, returned in the gathering dusk to the Station Hotel there to be greeted by the jolly proprietor and his wife.

Their humour and general bonhomie lifted our low spirits and the fine meal followed by a steaming hot pudding revived our flagging weary bodies. The stairs and the endless passages we had gone along in the Hall had taken it out of us, but we were returning back to our normal selves by the minute.

Holmes opened up a little after the rest by the fire and a glass of the local brew. He began to think out aloud, using me as usual as a sounding board to bounce off ideas and theories.

'As I said before, Watson, it may be difficult to prove it is a confidence trick, but well-nigh impossible to prove it is genuine.

'The Prime Minister will expect a definite answer one way or the other. I am beginning to smell the unpleasant odour of failure. I feel it in my bones, Watson, I really do.'

I had never known Holmes in this mood so early in a case. He always enjoyed the challenge. The more impossible the odds, the greater he enjoyed the case. Then I remembered the words the Prime Minister had spoken about this being much, much more serious than the missing Bruce-Partington naval plans. The balance of world power could be altered and Britain and the Empire threatened.

It was a heavy responsibility to place

on his shoulders, and one I knew I could do little to share. That evening, Holmes continued expanding upon the subject. Holmes considered, rightly so, that the first law of the hunter is to know all about the hunted. This is of course the basic law of all poachers. To know the habits and ways of all the creatures he wishes to take.

I remember as a boy being given a demonstration by the most skilled poacher I was ever to have the pleasure of knowing. I watched from the cover of the hedge as he walked across a grass field where, in the centre, a hare crouched. He did not approach the hare directly, but walked in a direction which gave the hare the impression it had not been seen and, provided it remained still, was safe.

As the poacher passed the point nearest to the hare, he took off his jacket and placed it in a bundle so the hare could observe it. Then he continued walking on well past the hare, but began to swing around in a curve, so eventually he was approaching the hare from behind.

The hare was now confused. It observed

the jacket on the ground as a threat, but before it could make up its mind about the approaching danger from the rear, the poacher had pounced, and had the hare quickly despatched.

I digress, but I have always considered that Holmes too was a poacher, but on a higher plane. He considered that, as no clues had as yet been obtained, knowing more about Rodger Hardy would not be unhelpful.

The person who knew more about him than anyone was Sir Simon, so on returning to Baker Street a meeting was arranged with him.

★ ★ ★

The following evening saw Holmes and me being welcomed into the home of Sir Simon. It was situated in one of London's most desirable areas, a typical town house of Georgian elegance, with interior furniture and soft furnishings to complement it. A comfortable drawing-room with a welcoming fire was the scene of our meeting.

Holmes soon outlined why he had wanted the meeting, and Sir Simon saw the logic of it and agreed to help.

'Well, pray, where shall I begin? You want me to give you a picture of the man, what his ambitions are, is he trustworthy? Do I think it is in his nature to mount what could be nothing more than a huge confidence trick, and lastly what appears to be his philosophy?' He looked from one to the other of us.

Holmes took the opportunity to encourage him. 'Just talk about him, the picture of the man will emerge. It will be easier that way.'

Sir Simon looked keenly at Holmes. Then the professional politician came to the fore.

'Rodger Hardy,' he began, 'was always well liked. I don't think he ever crossed swords with anyone in the whole time I knew him at university. He was the kind of man who, if he couldn't say a good thing about a person, then he wouldn't say anything. He was always one for a joke and a bit of horseplay, but it was never in spite, of course. He could take a joke too, and laugh about it.

'In debate he would put forward original ideas and surprised many of us with the depth of his thinking. He had an inventive mind; it was a family trait.

'He didn't seem to have changed much in his outlook and manner over the years and I found it easy to take up our friendship again, almost as though the years between had never been.

'His philosophy of life had been conditioned by what he had seen around the world. The cruelties and ill-treatment, to and by people, and the same cruelty extended to animals. The wickedness and injustices he had witnessed had made him wonder, he said, why one person has a happy, interesting and useful life, whilst another is born to dread each waking day, and has to carry that burden to the end of their lives, experiencing none of the pleasures and comforts of life that others take for granted.'

Sir Simon looked at us both in turn. 'I am sure we have all had those same thoughts, but have never expressed them. One evening after dinner when we were both well into the frame of mind when friends reveal their deepest private thoughts, Rodger remarked, 'Have you ever wondered why the Great Creator decided, after hundreds of millions of years, when only plant and animal life had inhabited the earth, why he chose to create mankind? Was it, do you think, that only He, the Great Creator, was at that time able to appreciate the beauty and glory of the morning sunrise and the magnificent skies of the setting sun? All the wonders of the forests and the lakes, and all the creatures that do dwell upon the earth?

' 'The swallow in the heavens, searching for insects in the air, is totally unaware of the mole tunnelling below the surface of the ground in search of worms. Likewise, the whale in the oceans is unaware of its land cousin, the elephant, in deepest Africa. Only man has this knowledge and more. Only man can appreciate what a wonderful world we inhabit.

' 'Sadly, only man has done more to alter the Creator's paradise than any other creature.' Only man, he said, was capable of destroying it all. Man must learn that we are custodians only, and that we own nothing; the poor man in his cottage, the Duke his estate, we are all mere custodians.'

Sir Simon took the poker and pushed back a log that threatened to fall from the fire into the hearth and said, 'I notice you smoke, Mr Holmes — the nicotine stains, the slight cough.'

Holmes smiled and laughed. 'I see that I am not the only detective present.'

Sir Simon smiled. 'Just an observation, but I remember Rodger talking at some length about his own smoking, and his cough, which eventually prompted him to consult a Chinese doctor. He told Rodger that in his view smoking was most dangerous to one's health — 'Much smoke . . . no hope . . . no smoke . . . much hope,' was how he put it.'

'H'mm.' Holmes took out his cigarette case, looked at it thoughtfully, and replaced it in his pocket unopened. 'He may well have been correct.'

Sir Simon continued his painting of

Rodger Hardy. He had sketched out the outline, now he was putting in a little detail.

'Rodger Hardy was deeply concerned about humanity, about the creatures who share the world with us . . . ' but before he could continue with the finer detail, Holmes interrupted him.

Holmes leaned forward. 'Then why do you think he wants one million pounds for his plans of the 'Transposer'? It hardly seems to go hand in hand with the picture you have given us.'

Sir Simon looked a little hurt at the attack Holmes had made upon the person he still considered his friend. His voice took on a tone of hostility. 'Why, it is obvious to me, if you knew him personally you would not ask that . . . he wanted it to give away. He wanted it to help those he saw as in the most need. Not to appear the great benevolent benefactor . . . that was not his style, but to give anonymously.'

Holmes asked, 'Have you proof of his act of anonymous help? This generosity of nature?'

I smiled inwardly at Holmes's breach of English, but neither Holmes nor Sir Simon seemed to have noticed it.

Sir Simon stared hard at Holmes and said quietly, 'Yes, I have; two cases in fact. One occurred when he was at university. It was not a gift of money, because he had very little of that then, but in a considerate act that helped a desperate student. I was the unseen witness. The second occasion was to help a colleague of mine who was also a friend of Rodger's. He saved him from financial ruin, although for over five years he was unable to repay the debt because Rodger had just vanished again.

'I agree this help was not given anonymously, but Rodger never spoke of it to anyone. I would not have known, had my friend not revealed who had saved him.

'You see, Rodger was a very successful business man. He made considerable monies from his inventive mind. For instance, he might come across in his travels a factory making a particular product. But, by installing a manufacturing method used in often a completely different industry, he was able to offer the owner a considerable saving in his production costs, and thus an increase in profits.

'As he went around the world, he found this to be so time and time again. Being an engineer with a flexible innovative mind, he could see at once how an improvement could be made.

'Rodger could, I am sure, have been a millionaire many times over had he chosen, but he had no desire to accumulate wealth just for the sake of it.'

Holmes leaned back into the comfort of his chair and said, 'If every man and woman had his philosophy in life, how much better a place this world of ours would be. Thank you, Sir Simon. I now have a better understanding of Rodger Hardy.'

He looked very serious as he held out his hand. 'Now, Sir Simon, we must be going and we thank you for your hospitality. I will keep you informed of events.'

I thought this unlikely, as Holmes was one to keep things very much to himself until he had tied a case up.

Sir Simon saw us out and as we walked down the road to get a cab, Holmes remarked how he felt more and more that the case would be difficult. 'Nay, perhaps impossible, Watson, and yet . . . ' He left the sentence unfinished and lapsed into silence as our boots rang out from the wet pavement.

'Let us walk home, the air is fresh after the rain, it will do us good.' I agreed with Holmes. After sitting so long it was good to exercise the legs and get the circulation going again.

\* \* \*

That evening Holmes again used me as a sounding board for some of his theories and the seemingly endless possibilities of the case.

'We must never lose sight of the fact,' Holmes said, 'that all the time dedicated men and women with brilliant minds are today building upon the discoveries of the past. Refining past theories and pushing the frontiers of science further and wider. You are aware of this as well as I am.'

'Yes,' I replied and feeling I too would like to expound my knowledge and perhaps even impress Holmes, I said, 'Did you know that atomic theory was first taught by the philosopher Leucippus of Miletus in the fifth century BC? His pupil Democritus said of the wind, that it enacted great force, but cannot be seen and the invisible spread of odours, sound and heat must be made up of particles too small to be seen by the human eye.'

I warmed to my subject. 'Clothes, he said, became wet by the rain, the sun dries them again. Therefore we must conclude the drops have been dissolved into small particles.' I felt proud of my little contribution.

Holmes clapped his hands together. 'Well done, Watson, I am impressed and for the record, I was not aware of those facts. However, Watson, the brief is to prove or disprove the possibility of transposing solids into a form whereby they can travel through the air and then re-form into their original state. Let us look at more recent scientific discoveries which might have, however remote, a bearing on the case for transposing solids.

'For instance, Wilhelm Konrad Roentgen found that X-rays have very great penetrating power. He found that X-rays travelled in straight lines and were not deflected in passing through electric or magnetic fields. And you will recall, Watson, that Pierre and Marie Curie have recently discovered two other radioactive elements polonium and radium.'

Holmes tipped backward in his chair and reached a book from the bookcase behind him. He thumbed through several pages before finding what he was looking for.

'Listen to this, Watson. In the preface to the fifth edition in 1893 John Tyndall states, 'Daily and weekly from all parts of the world I receive publications bearing upon the practical applications of electricity. The telephone, telegraph, electrical illuminations. Certainly Faraday could have had little notion of what his discoveries were capable of.'

'This bears out what I have just said. Because here in Europe and America we have no knowledge of transposing solids it does not mean that in the vast area of China, where little is known, Transposition has not been discovered.' He closed the book and replaced it.

I brought up another subject. 'What about 'Teleportation'? Now that has been a mysterious phenomenon which has baffled learned men for centuries. People claim to have moved through time and space to reappear thousands of miles, or sometimes just a few yards, from where they originally were.

'There was the case of Sister Mary of Agreda in Spain, who claimed to have travelled through time to spread Christianity to the heathen natives in Central America. This was in the sixteenth century. Of course at the time she was disbelieved and her account outraged her superiors.'

'And had she not been a nun, would surely have been burnt at the stake as a witch,' exclaimed Holmes. I agreed and continued.

'However, Father Alonzo de Benavides confirmed to both the Pope and King Philip IV of Spain that a mysterious nun, dressed in blue, had distributed rosaries and crosses among the natives.

'On his return to Spain, Father Benavides spoke with Sister Mary and fully supported her story. He was able to confirm, Holmes, astonishing details of people and places she spoke of, even though the convent testified she had never been absent. There was much more if I remember rightly, so much so, that this mystic phenomenon is considered unparalleled in the entire history of the world.'

'Amazing, Watson.' He was silent for a while. Then said, 'This is not a case of Teleportation, but of a prophetic dream, Watson. It was to do with the assassination of Prime Minister Spencer Perceval on May 11th, 1812. It concerned a mining manager, a Mr John Williams of Redruth, Cornwall. Eight days earlier Mr Williams had dreamed that he was in the lobby of the House of Commons, a place he had incidentally never visited in real life. In his dream, he was aware of a man wearing a green-coloured coat with metal buttons. A few moments later another man came into the lobby, whereupon the other man shot him.

'So vivid was the dream that it woke John Williams up and, waking up his wife, he described the dream to her, but his wife did not share the horror of the dream and so dismissed it, as indeed most of us would. During the same night, he was to have the same event in detail again in two further dreams.

'The next day, so upset by the dreams he had had, he could not help but discuss them with all and sundry. He did not, of course, know Spencer Perceval by sight and knew little of his politics. His son-in-law did know; he felt sure who the victim was: the Prime Minister.

'John Williams was inclined to go up to London and warn the Prime Minister, telling him about the shocking dream he had had, but his family talked him out of it, saying he would be ignored.

'In fact he would have been received very seriously, as the Prime Minister all week had been haunted by a premonition that he would be killed. He had told his wife about it, and on the night of May 10th he had dreamed about it, and it was almost identical to that of John Williams. A man wearing a green coat with brass buttons. It, too, had been so vivid that he had told the Earl of Harrowby about it, who had advised him not to go to the Commons that day.

'However, he ignored that advice and perhaps with misgivings, we can only assume, was rushing through the Commons to cast a vote, when a man wearing a green coat with brass buttons stepped out and pointing a gun at him, shot him dead. Of course, John Williams bitterly regretted that he had not followed his first inclination and gone up to London and warned the Prime Minister of his dream.

'A few weeks later he did visit the House of Commons, pointing out the exact spot where it happened. It is still a mystery today why this stranger to the Prime Minister should have this prophetic dream which tragically came so true.'

Holmes took hold of the poker and broke up a large piece of coal, to make it burn better. 'Unfortunately, Watson, the Teleportation is concerned with people, and belongs to the realm of the occult, whereas our problem is with the scientific.'

The broken-up coal burst into flame and Holmes continued to examine the case.

'Why did Rodger Hardy go over Halam Hall afterwards with a fine-tooth comb to remove every shred of evidence?' He looked at me.

'If he has perpetrated a gigantic confidence trick, then he wanted no clue as to how it was carried out to be found.'

Holmes added, 'Equally, of course, if the thing is genuine, he would want to leave no clue which might lead to the discovery of its secret.'

I added quickly, 'And I suppose the same reasoning can be used on why the junk sailed away, giving no one a chance to inspect it further.'

Holmes agreed, adding, 'And the wooden poles supporting the copper wire were a charade to mislead investigators. The means of how transposition actually is achieved could have been built into the junk, and therefore it was essential to remove it from prying eyes.'

Holmes was silent for some time, rubbing his long chin, then suddenly looking at me exclaimed, 'How other than 'transposition' could that huge wooden junk weighing thirty or forty tons, have been removed from that underground tomb?

'Sir Simon observed it being built month after month. Vast amounts of timber were used, fresh supplies arriving weekly were stacked around the walls, work benches, tools, shavings, sawdust, evidence enough of construction on a grand scale. The village people witnessed huge traction engines pulling loads of supplies to the Hall. Yet in less than two hours, it had vanished through thin air. You and I can vouch that the walls, ceiling and floor were solid concrete.' He seemed to slump back into his chair.

'We appear to be faced with a feat which defies normal logic or understanding. Again, we must fall back on the old axiom, that when all other contingencies fail — in this case, our investigation and the minds of learned scientists — whatever remains, however improbable, must be the truth. In this case, the discovery in China of the means of 'Transposition' is fact, but impossible to prove without the scientific knowhow.'

It was a glum pair of gentlemen Mrs Hudson found when she brought in our evening drink. Sensing our mood, Mrs Hudson withdrew, quietly closing the door behind her.

★ ★ ★

The next morning, to make matters worse, I received a telegram informing me that I was urgently needed by a patient who was very ill. He now lived in Brighton since his retirement. He would have no other doctor but me,

73

so I was obliged to be away at a time when I considered Holmes needed my support most.

It was with a heavy heart and a troubled mind that I reluctantly bid my old friend goodbye. I felt awful, I was letting him down. Not that I would be able to contribute much in the way of help, but I would be there to give my moral support.

Yet, what could I do but answer the call of my patient? I had become his doctor by one of those quirks of life we nearly all experience at some time or other.

It had occurred soon after Holmes and I decided to take the rooms at 221B Baker Street. Just like I had bumped into Stamford, my old dresser under me at Bart's, and who had been instrumental in bringing Holmes and I together, so it was that I acquired a patient.

I had been about to cross the road and was waiting for the traffic to pass, when I received a tap on the shoulder and, upon turning around, was overjoyed to discover an old friend, 'Trimmer'

Timmons; beaming face and as jovial as ever.

He was nicknamed Trimmer because of his insistance of trimming every vestige of fat from any meat he ate; bacon, beef, mutton, pork, whatever, with great deliberation, as though working on a cadaver.

He detached every morsel of fat, pushing it to one side of his plate, then satisfied that all that remained was lean, he would begin to eat. So Trimmer it became and Trimmer it remained at least in all his student days.

We both enjoyed meeting each other again, swapping anecdotes about our student days together at medical school and later at Netley, the course for Army surgeons.

He and I travelled together on the same troopship on the long voyage to India. It was a wonderful adventure for us both. For me, the Army posting was a godsend, far better than putting up a brass plate and sitting in a cold room somewhere, waiting and hoping some patient would come; starvation and penury was the lot of many newly qualified doctors, unless you were very fortunate.

It was not so with Trimmer, however. His father had a thriving practice in Brook Street. He had expected, nay insisted, that when Trimmer qualified he should join him in the practice.

But Trimmer had enjoyed his freedom for too long as a student, and was reluctant to be bound up in the strict and rigid life his father would demand, as essential to the professional niceties he considered his patients expected.

So after many family arguments about his future, Trimmer got his way and was allowed to have his freedom, for a short time, as an Army surgeon.

Having got the wanderlust out of his system, Trimmer returned and joined his father in the practice. None too soon either, because his father's health began to cause concern and he would often take to his bed for a few days, leaving Trimmer to manage on his own.

So over coffee Trimmer asked if I would locum at the times when his father took to his bed. I agreed, because although I had my Army pension it was not great, and any means I had of supplementing it was not to be overlooked.

So, soon afterwards I received a note from Trimmer asking me if I would locum for a day or two. This I did gladly, and that is how Mr James Henshaw of James Henshaw and Sons, Purveyors of High Quality Foods, became my patient.

He had never had need of a doctor in his life. His wife and sons likewise. Some families are like that, enjoying good health always, and unable to understand why others are not so blessed. As Trimmer put it, 'If every family were like them, doctors would sit on the pavements with begging bowls.'

But to Mr James Henshaw came an unusual experience; he became ill — suddenly. Trimmer was out doing the domiciliary rounds, and I had just finished the surgery when a cabby came demanding a doctor come at once, as Mr Henshaw of James Henshaw and Sons, Purveyors of High Quality Foods, was standing in his office, unable to move his legs. 'It's as though 'e's rooted to the floor, I seed 'im wi' me own eyes,' gasped out the excited cabby.

Grabbing my medical bag, I informed the nurse where I was going, and in a flash the cabby whipped up the horse and, in what seemed no time at all, I was being led through the doors of a very high-class emporium indeed.

The several shop assistants, men and women, attired in smart immaculate dress, broke off from serving, to stare at me as I rushed up the wide impressive staircase to his office.

I was shown in by an elderly lady clerk. I saw my patient at once; he was standing with his legs astride, grasping with both hands the side of his large leather-covered desk. He was truly transfixed, unable to move either leg even an inch. He looked at me with wide appealing eyes, rather like a lost dog who looks up at every stranger, hoping that it is its master.

He was sweating and had a terrified look upon his smooth plump face. A man of about sixty years of age, I guessed.

My first task was to calm him down

and so I talked and assured him that, as soon as I was able to examine him, I was sure he would soon be on the way to recovery. One of his sons had arrived, and had obviously been informed about the situation, because he had not interrupted my conversation between me and his father, but had stood quietly but concerned in the background.

I asked that we be left alone whilst I examined him. As I did so, I talked and discussed it with him. Soon the look of terror and despair was replaced by calm and, I think, hope that his condition was not life threatening. I explained he had an inguinal hernia, a rupture, and that palliative treatment was to wear a truss. I did not go further into the cause or description of a hernia, because I realised it would only upset my patient further.

Slowly, on its own accord, the hernia receded and my patient was able to begin moving his legs again, until he was able to take a few steps across the room and sit down in his chair.

With the help of his son, we supported him down the staircase and through the shop into a cab. His son and I accompanied him home, a rather grand house as would befit a successful purveyor of High Quality Foods.

After suggesting he take the rest of the day quietly at home and that I would see him the following day, I left him in the care of his loving family.

I became in his eyes the greatest doctor who walked, only because the man, never having any ill health, had no experience of the profession to compare me with.

Often patients, who are attended by one doctor all their lives, are very reluctant to have another, being certain that their doctor is the best in the world.

So grateful was my patient, that each Christmas I would receive a huge hamper containing a goose, wines, nuts and lots of other good things along with his best wishes. I must confess I felt quite a fraud, knowing I had performed no life-saving feat or anything special that any other doctor would not have done. But, as Holmes remarked, it obviously gives him great pleasure to give and I should be pleased it gave him such pleasure. I know Mrs Hudson agreed with that sentiment.

And so it was that I arrived in Brighton. I had hoped it was to be only a short stay and my ministrations would soon have my patient fit and well again. I was disappointed. I found him a very sick man, and his health was slow to recover.

I spent many restless nights wondering how Holmes was coping. Had he found some clue which would enable him to begin the jigsaw which, when completed, would enable him to meet the Prime Minister with a definite answer?

Yet the more I turned the case over in my mind, the more I considered Rodger Hardy was no confidence trickster. He had achieved a result which defied all known laws. No other conclusion could be reached. I remembered Sir Simon quoting his headmaster's report on Rodger Hardy, sneaked, he said, along with his own, when he was left alone in his study for a few minutes. 'High powers of concentration when his interest is aroused. Strong sense of duty.

Good sport. Will be greatly missed.' The character of a boy does not change so much when he becomes a man.

I felt great relief when my patient was sufficiently strong for me to leave him in the care of a dedicated nurse, enabling me to take the first available train up to London.

I had been away almost a month and it was with some trepidation that I arrived at Baker Street and sought from Mrs Hudson the state of health and general well-being of my friend, Holmes.

I was much relieved when she said he was 'Now his usual self' and continued, 'But he must be very busy as he was hardly ever in his rooms except to return and sleep.'

I asked her about what she meant by the expression. 'He was now his usual self'?

'Well,' she said, 'After you went away for the first few days he appeared most unlike his usual self. He would return in the evening for his meal looking most depressed, in fact as though he had all the worries of the world upon his shoulders. Then one evening he returned and appeared more cheerful playing his favourite pieces on his violin.' She smiled, 'I was sure he was all right again.'

I thanked her and, after dealing with my correspondence which had accumulated in my absence, I settled down to await the return of Holmes, hopefully in time for our evening meal together.

He arrived early and I was pleased to see the account of his health and well-being given by Mrs Hudson was correct. He appeared full of vim and vigour and I was touched by his obvious and genuine pleasure at my return.

When I considered the time was appropriate, I approached him about the current case of Rodger Hardy.

He rested his chin on his hand as he was wont to do, choosing his words, I thought, carefully, and replied:

'It is going very well, Watson. I must admit to you, at one time I felt I was up against a brick wall, a scientific brick wall. If I could have travelled to China and have spoken the tongue, moved about and investigated, then things might have been easier, much, much easier. But that was impossible.

'However, I hope shortly to be able to give a definite answer to Lord Bellinger. You know, it was my dread that I would have to face him with an indecisive answer. I would have failed him, myself and the country. The only real advantage I had in the case was the time element. Rodger Hardy had not pressed for an early decision, and had decided to visit America in the meantime. He is due back shortly.

'Rodger Hardy had realised the matter would have to be discussed eventually by the full Cabinet, and perhaps committees appointed, all of course sworn to secrecy, to discuss it before any decision was reached. Even with the full authority of the Prime Minister, it would all take time. Rodger Hardy had, however, put a deadline on the time; that time is almost up.'

He smiled at me and placed his hand on my shoulder.

'Now, Watson, my old friend. Enough

of the Rodger Hardy case, let me hear all the news you must have; about your patient, who I assume is now on his way to a full recovery, and of Brighton and its society, but most of all about yourself.'

I knew that he would reveal nothing more about the case and so we passed the evening in a relaxing way, after I had first brought him up to date about the health of my patient and the social events and news of Brighton.

I read the back issues of the London papers and caught up with the latest events, gossip and society functions, whilst Holmes tinkered with his test tubes and chemicals.

And so we settled back into our normal way of life at Baker Street, the excellent Mrs Hudson looking after us both in a way which bordered on that of a mother and an indulgent aunt.

It was two weeks after I had returned to Baker Street when Holmes, who had spent most of those two weeks out and about, obviously working on the Rodger Hardy case, asked if I was doing anything in particular the following afternoon. I replied that I was not. Holmes then surprised me by saying, 'We must look smart tomorrow, Watson. We will be meeting the Prime Minister and some of his Cabinet.'

I was surprised, but no further explanation was forthcoming, and so two o'clock the following afternoon found Holmes and me waiting outside a rather shabby building, a disused workshop in fact, in one of London's less salubrious streets, for the appearance of the Prime Minister and some members of his Cabinet.

Three four-wheelers arrived carrying the Prime Minister and three members of his Cabinet, which included Sir Simon, of course. In the other two coaches were a number of hefty policemen.

The Prime Minister seemed in a less sombre mood than the last time we had met, the Cabinet members likewise. The reason, I was to learn later, was that Holmes had promised the Prime Minister to end the uncertainty about the 'Transposer', and was prepared to prove his findings. The party followed

Holmes into the building, the policemen on guard outside.

The workshop was divided into three rectangular areas and had been built in the early eighteenth century, stone walls and roofed in Welsh slate. The three workshops were identical in size and layout, being, as I have mentioned, rectangular in shape. All three were connected by a corridor to allow passage from one workshop to another. A further door in each workshop allowed the workers to make use of the narrow piece of grass space between the buildings for the purpose of visiting the long since demolished wooden privies. The main reason for the space between the workshops, however, was to allow windows to be placed in every wall to make full use of the daylight.

Chairs had been arranged in a small office which was warmed by a blazing coal fire. Holmes later confessed that because of the years between the fireplace being used and now, the problem of removing birds' nests, soot and dislodged bricks had been a problem for one of the many casual workers whom Holmes employed from time to time. However, lighting the fire a few days before the visit had ensured there was no problem on the day.

Holmes cleared his throat as a means of showing his intention that he was about to explain the purpose of the visit.

'Prime Minister, gentlemen. In a few minutes I want to demonstrate, on a reduced scale of course, the sight which Sir Simon beheld in the underground ballroom of Halam Hall some weeks ago. The vessel you will observe is much, much smaller, but the principle of the arrangement is the same, being surrounded by posts and strands of copper wire, as was the junk at Halam Hall.

'You will hear the same noise of electrical generators as Sir Simon did. I give you the same warning too, as Rodger Hardy gave to Sir Simon: keep away from the copper wires and do not be tempted to touch the vessel by reaching between the strands of electric wire. If you follow these instructions, you will be perfectly safe. Would you kindly follow me?'

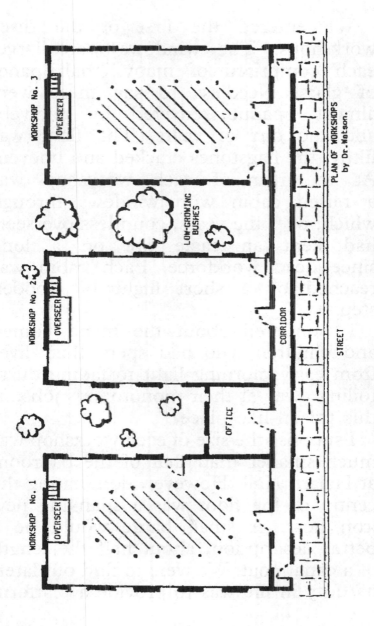

WORKSHOP No. 3

OVERSEER

WORKSHOP No. 2

OVERSEER

LOW-GROWING BUSHES

CORRIDOR

OFFICE

WORKSHOP No. 1

OVERSEER

STREET

PLAN OF WORKSHOPS
by Dr. Watson.

We entered the first of the three workshops. The windows were large, each comprised of many small panes of glass. Needless to say these were almost opaque, covered by cobwebs and the dirt of years. The floor was filthy, the flagstones cracked and uneven. At the rear of each workshop was a raised cabin with windows through which, over the years, countless overseers had kept an eagle eye on a long since dead workforce. Each cabin was reached by a short flight of wooden steps.

I wondered about the men, women and children who had spent their lives from early morning light to fading dusk, toiling away at their monotonous jobs, in this prison-like place.

I suppose the size of each workshop was much smaller than that of the ballroom at Halam Hall. However, dominating the centre of the floor was a spanking new iron boat. A small barge would be a better description, about half the length of a canal boat. We were to find out later, its duty in life was to provide a platform for workmen painting or repairing the sides of ships.

Around the boat were a number of upright posts supporting the copper wires, similar to those described by Sir Simon as seen around the Chinese junk in the ballroom.

I looked at the Prime Minister and compared the contrast between these squalid surroundings and those of No. 10 Downing Street.

I noted he was missing nothing and his eagle eyes were alert and searching as he walked slowly around, followed by Holmes and the three Cabinet ministers.

The Prime Minister, having completed his tour, stopped, turned around and faced Holmes, as if to indicate he had observed it thoroughly and awaited the next act of the play to unfold.

Holmes was at his best, dramatic and precise in his address. 'Gentlemen, you will observe the craft, which is known by the rivermen as a pontoon or lighter. It is used by workmen when painting or chipping rust from the sides of ships or carrying out repairs.

'You will observe it is newly built and is sporting a coat of black paint; for this is no pleasure craft, but is destined to a life of work and misuse. You will also observe that only by taking the roof off the building and lifting it out with a crane, can it be got out of the building, the windows and doors being far too small to allow exit.

'Listen also and you will hear the hum of the generators which, as we stand here at this very moment, are actually energising the vessel.'

We all listened and, true enough, the hum of the generators could be heard from somewhere in the building. Holmes continued, enjoying, I could see, every moment.

'Now, gentlemen, the energising process is about over and it is dangerous to be present when it actually transposes.' Holmes paused and looked at his watch. 'I have chosen an out of the way site on the Thames for the vessel to be transposed to and, if you will follow me, a short drive will take us to that place.'

Holmes again consulted his watch. 'Let us not delay, gentlemen. My calculation of the time required to transpose the vessel may be slightly incorrect.'

We hurried through the doorway with as much dignity as we could muster. I could not be but dismayed at the danger in which he had put the Prime Minister and all of us. But then, Holmes cared little for his own safety and assumed others were of the same opinion.

During the short drive in the four-wheeler I concluded that Holmes, with the help of Rodger Hardy by means of letter and wire to America, had put on this demonstration to prove to the Prime Minister and Cabinet members that the transposing of solids was possible, and the terms demanded by Rodger Hardy, one million pounds and the envelopes containing the secret plans to be distributed far and wide, only to be opened in the event of war, would have to be accepted.

The risk that Rodger Hardy would not make the same deal with foreign powers would have to be taken. But after all,

Rodger was British, his mother American, and despite his family's poor treatment in the past by an ungenerous government, Holmes must have felt sure he would do the honourable thing.

My thoughts were brought to a sudden end when the coach stopped. We had arrived at the rear of some old wooden warehouses by the side of the Thames. It was a well-chosen site; not a soul appeared to be about.

We alighted and the hefty policemen stationed themselves around so as to block off any casual intruders and, of course, were still completely unaware of the purpose of the visit.

We followed Holmes along a cobbled pathway by the side of the wooden warehouse and, turning the corner, looked down to see the lighter, pontoon, whatever you care to call it, tied up at the bottom of a flight of old stone steps. The slap, slap, slap of gentle waves were the only sounds which broke the silence.

We were initially shocked, amazed and not a little disturbed just as Sir Simon had been on that night at Halam Hall.

'My God!' and 'Incredible!' were just a few of the exclamations voiced. There was a feeling of fright and alarm amongst us. We didn't understand the means by which it had been transposed. It was unnatural. We were witnessing the birth of a new era.

The coming of the railways had ruined the canal trade: could this discovery herald the end of the railways, even ships, if the process could be made to operate over greater distances?

I confess I looked at the little vessel with anxious eyes. I was near the Prime Minister and overheard him say to Holmes, 'I don't like it. I don't like it one little bit.' He paused and again spoke to Holmes, and was overheard by us all to say, 'I don't know how you have managed in such a short number of weeks to set up this demonstration, but I must congratulate you. However, I had only wished that this . . . Rodger Hardy's 'Transposer' thing was . . . ' He paused and his countenance took on that old worried look . . . 'Yes, a fraud, a fake, and that it was all only a huge confidence trick for him to make easy money. This contraption will cause more problems to our national security than it will ever help. I predict it will begin an era of upheaval and uncertainty.'

Holmes smiled and replied, 'I should not make a judgement yet, Prime Minister; the demonstration I have put on is not yet over by a long chalk.' He chuckled, 'The best is yet to come.'

Lord Bellinger looked at Holmes with displeasure. He was not used to such cavalier repartee, especially in front of his ministers. He guessed Holmes was having a private joke at his expense, but the bait Holmes had thrown him and his attitude, although flippant, was not to be ignored.

Lord Bellinger drew himself up and gave Holmes his most scathing look. 'I do not quite understand that remark, Mr Holmes. If you have more to disclose, please do so.' I looked at Holmes and detected in his face the expression that he realised he had overstepped the mark with the elder statesman, and was duly chastened.

Unsmiling now, Holmes replied. 'Yes, I have further facts to disclose, and I hope more pleasing to you, Prime Minister. If you would be so good as to follow me and return to the old workshops again, I will reveal them.'

We took our seats once again in the four-wheelers. I noticed the puzzled looks on the faces of the policemen. Why, they must have wondered, should the Prime Minister and some of his Cabinet come to such a derelict part of London, to observe a lighter moored on the Thames at the bottom of some old steps? Knowing policemen and their habits, they had no doubt sneaked a look to try and discover what it was all about.

The Cabinet ministers sharing the four-wheeler with me didn't discuss matters, they seemed rather overawed by the whole affair. I was later to learn they had only become privy to the details a few days before and were still trying to digest the implications it could have on national security.

In no time at all we had arrived back at the old workshops. We filed in through the doorway, Holmes leading, followed by the Prime Minister, Sir Simon, the Cabinet ministers and myself, the policemen standing around outside on the pavement.

We entered the first workshop again where we had inspected the lighter. The lighter was gone. Only the wooden poles supporting the strands of copper wire remained.

Although we had only just left the little vessel tied up by the steps, it was still a shock to find it missing. I know I looked around at the windows and the roof confirming to myself the impossibility of taking out the vessel. We all tried to understand how the 'Transposer' was able to accomplish this miracle.

Lord Bellinger looked at Holmes and his expression said, 'Yes, I expected the place to be empty; we have just left it tied up on the Thames, so what are these new revelations?'

Holmes read the expression too. 'If you will follow me, sir.' Holmes led us out again along a passageway to the third workshop, ignoring the middle workshop.

The third workshop was identical in every way to the first one we had been in, but it was a shock to see the little vessel back again, just as in the first workshop, surrounded by wooden posts and copper wire.

I think we were all nonplussed at the turn of events. We seemed to be in a sort of Alice in Wonderland situation. Before anyone, even Lord Bellinger, could comment, Holmes said, 'Please, sir, gentlemen, would you follow me?'

The expression upon all our faces was one of utter confusion. As we followed Holmes up the steps leading to the overseer's observation cabin I felt a sort of mounting drama was about to be revealed. I was not wrong.

When we were all assembled, Holmes turned to the party and began.

'I think in the next fifteen minutes, Prime Minister and gentlemen, you will observe better than any way I could describe in words, what happened that evening at Halam Hall between the time Rodger Hardy and Sir Simon inspected the Chinese junk and when they returned two hours later.

'The Chinese junk was much larger and therefore the time took longer, whereas this vessel is much smaller and therefore will take much less time, a quarter of an hour perhaps. The method, though, is identical to that carried out at Halam Hall.'

Holmes paused and looked at his watch. 'It is a minute to the hour, gentlemen!' We waited, the suspense towards the end of that minute was indescribable. I reasoned that whatever Holmes had in store for us to observe, it could not compete with the present tension, but again I was wrong.

We saw Holmes step forward and strike a gong, a gong I had failed to notice before, and as the last of the sound faded away, the door at the far end of the workshop burst open and ten Chinamen with huge flashing machetes ran down the side of the vessel. One Chinaman pushed the poles and wires back against the walls. The others began slashing and demolishing the vessel. Under the weight of this onslaught, the sides of the vessel collapsed, the deck sagged. All this went on at a frenzied pace impossible to describe.

A few of the Chinamen were gathering up the pieces and were carrying them away through the connecting door into the middle workshop and so out of sight.

It seemed incredible that what had minutes before been a solid-looking brand-new iron vessel was collapsing before our eyes, as the Chinamen continued to slash, rip and carry away the huge chunks of cardboard and paper from which it was constructed.

We watched fascinated, spellbound would be a better description. I tore my eyes away for a moment from the noise and mayhem of the frenetic activity to stare at Lord Bellinger. I shall never forget the child-like look that the elder statesman had on his face. It was, I imagine, the joy of observing such unbounded energy being released and seeing the problem which had so wracked him over the past few weeks, dissolving before his eyes.

The fifteen minutes were almost passed away and the Chinamen were putting back into place the poles and wires again. The last scraps of paper and cardboard were swept from the floor. A few moments later and the Chinamen lined up at the far end of the workshop, bowed slowly from the waist and, grinning, filed out closing the door behind them.

The whole demonstration had been pure theatre. The build-up of the tension and expectation was superb, the following performance magnificent.

The look on the faces of all present was a sight I shall always remember. It had been said Lord Bellinger never smiled, didn't even know how to. Now his face was wreathed in them. He turned to Holmes and held out his hand. 'Mr Holmes, never in my whole life have I experienced an occasion remotely like this. Certainly I have never witnessed such a sight of sheer exuberant activity.'

Holmes smiled and shook the outstretched hand. 'I think we can all rest assured in our beds tonight, knowing the threat to

Queen and Empire is no longer with us from the Rodger Hardy 'Transposer',' replied Holmes.

The Cabinet ministers babbled and laughed like school children after seeing a pantomime as Holmes accompanied the Prime Minister to his coach.

The Prime Minister held out his hand once again, shook hands with Holmes, and then with me. 'Perhaps Mr Holmes and you, Dr Watson, will have dinner at No. 10 tomorrow, and afterwards, behind closed doors, my Cabinet colleagues and I might be given the facts of how you solved, what I must confess, appeared to be the unsolvable.' He put one foot on the step of the four-wheeler and turned towards Holmes. 'You and I, Mr Holmes, should exchange jobs.' He paused. 'But perhaps not; I would make a poor detective.' With a smile still lighting his face, he entered the four-wheeler followed by his ministers.

The policemen had that puzzled look still upon their faces, unable to understand what had been going on. They, of course, had been outside the building, guarding the entrance against any intruders, and were still not privy to anything. The few local people were puzzled too, no doubt, at the sight of the four-wheelers drawn up outside those old empty workshops being guarded by a posse of large hefty policemen. Had they known the Prime Minister was inside the building, a crowd would soon have gathered.

That evening Holmes and I discussed the events of the day, but not how he had achieved what had seemed the impossible. I was content to await the following evening when Holmes, in his inimitable manner, would, like a surgeon before a group of students, dissect a body step by step, the mysteries and functions of each organ explained in a logical and lucid manner.

★ ★ ★

We arrived at No. 10 the following evening and enjoyed a superb dinner in the most congenial surroundings, the glassware and silver picking up the light from the magnificent chandeliers. The walls were hung with wonderful paintings by the great artists of the past. Altogether a most memorable occasion, a reminder of the grand dinners held in the regimental mess I had attended in the past.

I knew, though, the best was yet to come. After the port was passed around, we retired to a comfortable room with sofas and easy chairs.

Lord Bellinger spoke first. 'I am sure we are all waiting with bated breath for you to reveal, Mr Holmes, how you brought this case, which let us not forget appeared such a threat, to a most successful conclusion.' He sank back into his chair displaying every indication of looking forward to hearing what Holmes had to reveal.

Holmes leaned forward, his eyes swiftly looking from face to face at his expectant audience, then began.

'When Dr Watson and I started the investigation, we went to Halam Hall, spending the day examining the ballroom, the Hall itself and then the grounds. As my old friend Inspector Lestrade of the Yard would say, it was as clean as a whistle. There was hardly a sign of what had taken place there, not one single clue remained which might have led us on to another.

'Rodger Hardy had made good use of the time to clean up the place between that weekend, when he put on his superb demonstration for Sir Simon, and the time we began our investigation. Two weeks in fact had passed.

'The following days I decided to try and trace the Chinese junk. After all a Chinese junk on the River Thames is not exactly an everyday sight. Again I drew a blank. I was to learn later from my Chinese friends that they had hidden it during the daylight hours after Sir Simon's inspection and, during that night, had sailed it laden with heavy stone ballast, out to sea and sank her. They returned to shore in a small rowing boat.

'I should like to point out that I had been without the invaluable help given me on most of my cases by Dr Watson. He had been called away to Brighton to attend an old patient. I can assure you he was sorely missed.'

They acknowledged this statement by looking towards me for a moment, before turning once again to listen to Holmes. I felt a great warmth towards my old friend and have to acknowledge a smarting in my eyes.

'I made enquiries then from electrical engineering firms from whom Rodger Hardy might have obtained his electrical apparatus. Here I was more fortunate. It seemed to confirm Rodger Hardy's account of his work on developing the 'Transposer' with the scientists in China.

'Over the past years the firms had despatched electrical goods to him in China, and over the last few months had delivered similar equipment to Halam Hall.

'I reasoned, then, that the Chinese junk and her crew may have been on the high seas on their way back to China. However, I decided that if they were not, then the most obvious place they might be found was here in London's Chinatown.

'As Dr Watson is aware, I have a great many friends in that oriental part of London, so I had them put the word about. Results were spectacular. I found my ten Chinamen; they were the key to enable me to unlock the whole mystery. Posing as an intimate friend of Rodger Hardy, and using the subterfuge of wanting to win a bet against my friends, I was to discover all I wanted to know.

'As we are all aware, the Chinese are great gamblers and I explained that I had bet my friends that I could also perform the magic trick of making a vessel vanish and reappear again. With the lure of gold sovereigns, I was able to learn unobtrusively how Rodger Hardy had worked his confidence trick which, I think we all must admit, was a piece of sheer brilliance.'

The Cabinet ministers nodded agreement and the Prime Minister added his approval too.

'I felt on learning all the facts that

108

it wouldn't be sufficient to be able to explain the confidence trick in words; much better and more effective to put on a demonstration. However, I reasoned it would need to be on a smaller scale, both size of the vessel, reduced, and the time taken to construct them. I say them, because I had decided to have two identical cardboard vessels made. More of that later.

'The story I obtained from the China-men over many cups of tea and numerous visits was as follows. Rodger Hardy had bought the newly built junk in China. He had hired five experienced seamen to sail the craft across the world to Britain. The other five Chinamen were craftsmen in the art of making objects of everyday use such as a bed, table, chair, desk, rickshaws and even small houses; all made from paper and cardboard, to be burned at the funerals of rich Chinese.

The models are life sized and so realistic that, it is said, they are impossible to distinguish from the real thing. Burning these objects at a funeral is thought to enable the deceased to arrive in the afterlife with essential goods to begin again. To cut a long story very short, Rodger Hardy, with the lure of much gold, and the promise of more when the job was done, persuaded the ten Chinamen to leave their homeland and sail to the land of the 'long-nosed devils' as white men are called in China.

'The five craftsmen would labour on the journey to help sail the craft under the direction of the experienced seamen, cooking the meals, pulling on the ropes and in general making themselves useful.

'Of course the roles were reversed when they reached Halam Hall. The craftsmen set about making a copy of the junk whilst the seamen made themselves useful, cooking and helping in any way they could.

'The Chinamen knew nothing, of course, of the real reason why the strange long-nosed Englishman should want to do this unusual thing to win a bet, but you must remember stories about the strange ways of Europeans, especially the British, had filtered for years back to China.

'So the Chinese junk duly arrived at the mouth of the Thames and was met by a river pilot, who had been handsomely paid by Rodger Hardy, to be on the lookout for just such an arrival. Suitably disguised, with mast and rattan sail hidden under tarpaulins, she was towed to a preselected covered-in boathouse. There to await her brief appearance when Sir Simon would inspect her, then down to the sea and sunk, a few months later.'

Holmes reached out, took up his glass and sipped slowly. I looked at his attentive audience, rather like children being told a story, spellbound and waiting to hear more, I thought. Holmes put down his glass and continued.

'We must remember, Halam Hall is rather isolated and the only staff was a cook and her daughter, both of whom lived in the village, and an elderly gardener who came daily, also from the village. Plus a young stable boy. The young lad lived over the stable and looked after the horse and drove the dogcart; he helped the gardener too. On a later visit to Halam Hall, I spoke to them all in turn except the stable lad, who had by then joined the Army. They all remarked that the Chinamen kept very much to themselves and confirmed what I had already gathered, that Rodger Hardy was a fine gentleman, considerate and generous. When he closed the Hall and put it up for sale, he gave them all a handsome present of money as a way of showing his appreciation of them.

'The village people told of loads of wood and strange objects being delivered by steam traction lorries from time to time, passing through the village on the way up to the Hall.

'From my Chinese friends I found out that when Rodger Hardy first showed Sir Simon the keel and ribs of the junk, they were of genuine wood. But the heavy baulks of timber which you saw, Sir Simon, making up the keel, were in fact only thin planks, made to appear like thick heavy oak timbers.

'On your second visit a month later, and you again inspected the progress which had been made of the building of the junk, again you could touch and see it was definitely wood. The sawdust, offcuts of wood and shavings, all went to confirm this. However, between that second visit and third visit, the keel and wooden ribs of the vessel had been taken away and the cardboard and paper construction replaced it.

'They obstructed, with timber and tools, the foot of the stairs leading into the ballroom, making it difficult for you to inspect the hull closely. The lighting was not good either; several of the lamps were unlit. Rodger Hardy had made the excuse that he was having trouble with them, I believe.' Holmes looked at Sir Simon who nodded agreement.

Holmes continued. 'Rodger Hardy had chosen you, his witness, very well.' He again looked towards Sir Simon and said, 'Sir Simon, like many, no doubt, of the Cabinet, is not remotely aware of the ways men work wood with axe, saw and plane. The shavings, sawdust, wood and tools lying around were enough to give the impression and create the illusion that what you were seeing was a vessel made of solid English oak, and having been given a brief view of the month's progress, there your interest ended.

'Now had you, Sir Simon, been a carpenter, or a craftsman of any kind, you would have been sufficiently interested in another's craftsmanship to observe it closer and perhaps ask questions about its construction.'

Holmes uncrossed his long legs again, took another sip from his glass and continued. 'Rodger Hardy relied upon this very fact. He might have chosen a friend or acquaintance from the civil service, the admiralty, or parliament, to be a witness, but when he heard that his old university friend was now a member of the Cabinet he concluded he could find no better person.

'Relying upon Sir Simon's lack of curiosity and interest in all things of a technical nature, he was able to impress him with a glimpse of electric cables, dials and switches. To add further authenticity to the occasion, he rigged up a simple mechanical device which, when turned by hand, by one of the Chinamen in this case, gave a humming sound easily mistaken for an electrical generator. The driving power for the generators was supposed to be provided by two hired steam tractors, but only their noise, and the hiss of steam, was really needed to create the illusion.

'Of course, Rodger Hardy was aware that any investigating team coming to Halam Hall would want to know how the generators were powered. The two steam-tractor drivers made great play of obtaining water from the village pond, both on the day before the demonstration, and on their departure next day. Thus the village people would provide ample verification of how steam tractors were seen to have been used at the Hall on the evening in question.

'The posts and strands of copper wire around the vessel were intended to both impress Sir Simon that it was essential to the transposition process, and to prevent him, after being warned of the danger, from reaching between them and touching the vessel, perhaps to admire the smoothness of the paintwork, thus discovering it was constructed only of paper and card. All part of the elaborate deception.

'After Sir Simon had walked around the vessel and had withdrawn with Rodger Hardy to partake of dinner, the same frantic activity took place you witnessed yesterday in the workshops. This time, of course, the Chinese junk was much, much larger and the time allowed for dismantling it had to be greater.

'Dinner was an ideal length of time to execute the dismantling of the vessel. After about two hours and following a good meal and suitably good wines Rodger Hardy was ready to spring his ingenious confidence trick.

'Just before the estimated time when he was to take Sir Simon back to the ballroom, he excused himself for a few minutes. This would be to make sure all was well and there were no last-minute hitches.

'The Chinamen had taken the paper and debris to one of the unused rooms nearby. Most probably the withdrawing-room. They disposed of it permanently the following day, after Sir Simon had

116

returned to London.'

Holmes turned to me and said, 'The reason why Dr Watson and I never found a trace of anything was because in the kitchen garden there was a disused well. Everything was thrown down it, and the top covered with wooden boards and earth. As a final touch, plants were carefully taken from other parts of the garden and replanted over the disturbed earth as camouflage.'

Holmes smiled when Lord Bellinger said, 'It is an incredible story of deception, Holmes, almost unbelievable,' shaking his head from side to side.

Holmes replied, 'I agree, Prime Minister. It was planned over a long time and masterfully carried out.'

Sir Simon leaned forward and tipped his drinking glass upside down to indicate it was empty. One of the other Cabinet members passed over the decanter. When all the glasses had been recharged, the Prime Minister asked:

'What I want to hear, Mr Holmes, is how you arranged to put on an almost identical demonstration of the one witnessed at Halam Hall.'

The others clamoured to hear the account too.

Holmes took a sip from his recharged glass and put it down with great deliberation onto the walnut occasional table by his elbow. We all waited with great expectation. We were not disappointed.

'I mentioned earlier how addicted to gambling the Chinese are. I was able to use this vice to advantage, saying that I too wished to gamble but, like my friend Rodger Hardy, wanted to make sure I would win. They laughed like young children being let into a secret. I explained that I too wanted to perform the magic trick and win much money from my friends which I would share with them. They would build me a small boat and I would bet my friends I could make it vanish. They fell about laughing and could not wait to begin making another paper and cardboard boat.

'I searched around for suitable premises and was fortunate in renting the three disused identical-sized workshops. They had small doors and a connecting corridor, although dirty and in a poor state of repair they would fulfil my purpose exactly.

'I looked then for a new suitably sized craft which could be copied. This proved more difficult. I was beginning to despair when I came across this pontoon which had just been built and was awaiting collection in a boat-builder's yard. I was able to persuade the owners to delay collection from the yard for a while by paying double the hiring fee they would normally charge when hiring it out.

'The Chinamen descended upon it like monkeys, examining and measuring every part of it. They were delighted when I presented them with a set of photographs I had had taken of the vessel, and they assured me having them would considerably speed up the time of construction. I decided to have two copies of the vessel made. One copy would be built in the first workshop, and the other in the third workshop.

'The middle workshop would make suitable sleeping and living accommodation and on the day of the demonstration would store all the debris of both demolished pontoons.'

Holmes continued his account before his spellbound audience. I smiled inwardly, knowing that it would be many a long year before, if ever, they would listen to such a fascinating story. Holmes smiled and, enjoying every moment, went on.

'I have not mentioned during all this account my very good friend, Mr Hing Sung. He acted as my interpreter during my negotiations with the Chinamen and throughout, supervising the copying and building of the pontoons. He will return to his laundry a much richer man, and the Chinese seamen and craftsmen will fade into the scene of London's Chinatown, also wealthier, to become part of this great city's society, enriching and adding to our national culture.'

Events explained by Holmes always seemed so simple, and one wonders why a case could have seemed so impossible to fathom, and yet have so simple an explanation. Yet I knew that it was his sheer brilliance which picked apart the facts of a case, found the vital clues and came up with a solution. Holmes remarked once that the fact magicians never revealed their secrets was because, once revealed, the audience would feel cheated, and illusion, which is the basis of all the aura of magic, would be eroded away, not to mention, he laughed, that the magician relied upon audiences night after night coming to see him for his bread and butter.

Holmes concluded, 'Those, Prime Minister, are the facts of the case. There is no 'Transposing Machine', no threat to Great Britain or the Empire. Rodger Hardy has a brilliant brain, and he is to be congratulated upon this attempt of what was a unique and imaginative means to get back money from a government who had reneged on his family, many years ago.

'But he failed, and failed because of one error, and that error was, he should never have allowed the Chinamen to settle here in London's Chinatown. Instead, suitably rewarded, he should have paid their fare back to China. Had he done this, I would never have had the opportunity of learning from them, first hand, how the confidence trick had been worked.

'But it was the lure of London's streets lined with gold which had persuaded them to sail halfway around the world to come here in the first instance. He saw no risk from ten Chinamen unable to speak English disappearing into the busy London scene.'

Holmes leaned back into his chair and, placing both his hands together to form a spire, indicated his explanation was finished. Lord Bellinger, I noted, made opposite body movements, he leaned forward and gripped the arms of his leather chair. He looked around at his Cabinet ministers, two of whom had hardly spoken at all, but to nod and make noises which indicated they were following every word with utmost interest. I think they were overawed by the whole affair. The masterly way Holmes had presented the facts had held them fascinated. Lord Bellinger spoke.

'Why, Mr Holmes, did Rodger Hardy choose to transpose a thing as bizarre as a Chinese junk as a means of perpetrating his confidence trick? For instance, he could have used a railway carriage or some similar large object?'

Holmes appreciated the thinking behind the question and his reply was a compliment to that thinking.

'I have given that very question much thought, sir, and I have come to this conclusion. Rodger Hardy wanted to construct, over many months, something substantial that could be seen in all its stages of building, until it was finally completed. A sailing vessel, he decided, would be ideal considering the fact that it would almost fill the ballroom, and could by no means be taken out whole, all exits being too small.

'Furthermore, a sailing vessel, the real one that is, would be easy to hide until required, and hidden again afterwards until sinking it later at night in the sea.

'It also had to be something which was not metallic. Wood is not a conductor of electricity, as you know. It would thus prove that any non-metallic material could be transposed.

'He wanted something unique, dramatic and utterly incomprehensible to baffle all reason and logic. What better vessel than a Chinese junk, surely never ever seen on the Thames or in the Western hemisphere before.'

The Prime Minister nodded his head several times whilst weighing up the various points Holmes had made. 'I agree with that reasoning. It does make sense. A remarkable affair altogether . . . a most remarkable affair indeed.' He looked at his three ministers and said, 'I have had a word with the Lord Chief Justice and reluctantly we agreed there is no way we can prosecute this scoundrel Hardy when he returns from America.'

They tut-tutted, but agreed.

Holmes, on the other hand, took us all by surprise by saying, 'I agree there is no way he can be prosecuted, having committed no crime, but instead, we should try and come to an agreement with him.'

We all stared at Holmes and tried to understand the logic of his statement. Lord Bellinger, now aware that Holmes was a player of much ability, smiled, remembering how Holmes had once before outmatched him.

'Now, Mr Holmes, what devious plan have you in that head of yours?'

'Well, sir, suppose we could persuade Rodger Hardy to take his 'Transposer' abroad to each of the major powers in turn. With, of course, the same restrictions, that only in the event of the outbreak of hostilities was it to be activated.'

The smile grew on Lord Bellinger's face as Holmes continued.

'It could alter the entire thinking of these major powers' generals and admirals when planning their future needs of guns and ships for their armed forces. It would give our own service chiefs a distinct advantage knowing the enemy were relying upon the help of a non-existent invention to move weapons of war about.

'As an inducement to Mr Hardy I would suggest a sum of fifty thousand pounds, and all the help we can give him in the way of language translators, letters of introduction and diplomatic embassy procedures. After his first success, with the equivalent of one million pounds in his account, all we need do is continue to help him sell his confidence trick to the next major power, and just sit back.'

Lord Bellinger shook his head from side to side, slapped his thigh and exclaimed heartily, 'Only you, Mr Holmes, I am sure, could have seen a means to use the 'Transposer' confidence trick to Britain's advantage.

'Why, without any extra financing, it could give our Army and Navy an overpowering advantage in the world. I look forward indeed to my next meeting with the service chiefs.'

One of the ministers, a dour, insignificant individual who had shown less enthusiasm about the achievements of my friend Holmes, spoke his views for the first time. 'I shouldn't be too optimistic, Prime Minister. We had not been hoodwinked by it, so why should other foreign powers not also see it for what it is, a cheap confidence trick?'

Lord Bellinger glared at the speaker

and in a tone which a master might address a rather obtuse pupil, replied, 'Because, minister, firstly, we as you put it, in spite of all the best minds and brains in the country could not categorically dismiss it as a genuine advance in the field of science. Secondly, we had the advantage of the service of Mr Holmes; other nations have not.'

Having duly administered his rebuke to the unfortunate minister, he turned to Holmes and said, 'However, I hate to see that scoundrel Hardy obtaining all those millions, in spite of the advantage it could bestow on this country.'

Holmes leaned forward, closer to Lord Bellinger. 'Does that matter, Prime Minister? It won't be costing the British taxpayer anything, will it?'

Lord Bellinger threw up his hands in feigned horror and cried, 'Is there no limit to your plotting devious mind, Mr Holmes? I am thankful you are not a member of my Cabinet or I should be fearful every day for my job.' He laughed until he had to wipe away the tears from his eyes.

Holmes was, by any standard, a giant even amongst these men.

'One last question, Mr Holmes. What do you think Rodger Hardy was doing all those years in China?'

Holmes spread out the fingers of his outstretched hands. 'Until he returns from America and I have an opportunity to speak with him, we can only assume he had spent his years following the profession he knew best, that of engineering.

'In many ways China has a culture which we in the West can only envy, but as regards engineering it is very backward. It would have been ideal territory for him to use his knowledge and talents.'

\* \* \*

And so ends my account of the Chinese junk, or almost . . .

Holmes and Sir Simon at a meeting with Lord Bellinger a few days later were able to improve the image the Premier held of Rodger Hardy, explaining his true motives behind the confidence trick.

'It was a matter of family honour,

Prime Minister, to even out the score against a government who in the past had been partly responsible in the bankrupting of his family. The money obtained, he would no doubt give to causes he considered worthy of charity.'

'You mean he is a sort of combined avenging angel and latter-day Robin Hood — good intentions if a bit unorthodox?'

Holmes smiled. 'Something like that, sir.'

Lord Bellinger reached out his arm and placed his hand on Holmes's shoulder. 'Now about a knighthood for exceptional services to the nation, surely this time you will accept it . . . ?'

# Sherlock Holmes and the Tick Tock Man

It began like any other morning lately, wash, shave and breakfast, then Mrs Hudson would bring in the morning papers and clear away the table. Only this morning, Mrs Hudson broke the cycle.

'Before you, Mr Holmes, and Dr Watson settle down to read the papers, I wonder if you would mind hearing a request I should like to make and discuss with you?' We leaned back into our chairs and bade her speak.

'Well, yesterday Mr Hudson and me received a letter from my sister who lives at Ilfracombe. She says now her youngest daughter is off their hands, she has a spare bedroom, and would we like to spend a couple of weeks' holiday with them?' She looked at us both and as neither of us commented, she hurried on, 'I could get a friend of mine to come and cook your breakfasts, and later on, cook your evening meal . . . but it would mean the place would be locked up and during the daytime of course . . . if any important clients called like . . . I wouldn't be here to take any messages . . . ' Her voice trailed off as she looked from one to the other of us with an appealing look.

The opportunity of a holiday by the sea was rare indeed for most people of her station. The added joy of the occasion was, it would enable her to see her sister again after many years' separation. I was about to reply when Holmes forestalled me.

'What a wonderful generous offer from your sister. Of course you and Mr Hudson must take advantage of this opportunity . . . it will do you both the world of good, won't it, Watson?' I, of course, agreed with him.

Holmes continued, 'Don't make any arrangements with your friend about cooking our meals until I have discussed the matter with Dr Watson, will you please . . . and Oh! I presume your sister has not specified any particular dates?'

'No, Mr Holmes. I suppose as the bedroom is vacant, we could go any time.'

'Very good, Mrs Hudson, and I am sure Dr Watson agrees with me that we are very happy for you.'

'Thank you very much, both of you. Mr Hudson will be so pleased.' She carried the tray with our used breakfast utensils out of the room and quietly closed the door behind her.

I was surprised at Holmes's seeming cheerfulness. I knew, of course, he would agree to our landlady's request, but it had also seemed to have had an uplifting effect upon him. A few moments later I was to discover why.

'What say we take a holiday, too?' He slid his chair under the table and crossed to the window, looked out and turned about to face me. 'Think about it, Watson. I have no case just now, your locum appointment is not until late September. Why should we not take the opportunity to holiday during the same weeks as Mrs Hudson?'

I must confess I was surprised. Holmes's suggestion took me aback for a few moments, but quickly considering it, decided it was a capital idea and said so.

'One thing though, where do we holiday?'

Holmes went over to the bookshelf and took down two books each containing a map of the British Isles. 'I think we should study the map and select a number of locations we feel we should like to visit. Then write their names on separate pieces of paper, put them in the time-honoured hat, and let fate choose for us in the form of our good landlady.'

After much study of our maps, this is what we duly did. Each one of us selected ten locations and when Mrs Hudson later tapped at the door to inform us she was away to do her shopping, all was ready to invite her to determine our fate, although I confess, the word fate seems inappropriate in context with holidays. I think she was quietly proud that she should be instrumental in choosing our holiday venue, and after being asked to select a piece of paper from my hat, read out the place name with a certain amount of importance, 'The surrounding countryside around Bakewell in the county of Derbyshire.'

It was not one of my chosen locations, but I was pleased all the same. I must confess I had not even considered it, knowing little about the county. When I confessed my ignorance to Holmes, he surprised me too, by admitting he also knew little about the county, and this was why he had included it in his locations.

'Now then, Mrs Hudson, would the next two weeks be convenient to you and Mr Hudson?' She was, like me, surprised at the speed at which things were happening. However, promising to write a letter to her sister accepting the invitation that very afternoon, we chose four days hence, a Saturday, to all begin our holidays.

'I shall, of course, arrange a watch by my Baker Street Irregulars on the premises during our absence, Watson.

Just to be on the safe side.' I was amused at Holmes's sudden energy and desire to go on holiday.

'Now I intend going out and buying us a map of the district and a new rucksack for each of us.'

'And I shall look up the Bradshaw to see about suitable trains and connections.'

'Excellent, Watson, excellent.' There was no doubt, we were both as excited over the proposed holiday as if we were two college students looking forward to some field work in their vacation.

On sorting out the railway travel, I found we were fortunate in that the Manchester, Sheffield and Lincolnshire Railway which had become the Great Central had, that very spring, extended their services to Marylebone. I remember it being reported in the papers with some pessimism at the time, some wit writing that if the old M.S. and L. stood for 'Money Sunk and Lost', G.C. clearly meant 'Gone Completely.'

However, as we were to discover a few days later, the Great Central London expresses had a high proportion of corridor coaches, smartly turned out and most comfortable. Our journey from Marylebone to Sheffield, a total of 164 miles, was covered in 192 minutes. From Sheffield I saw there were plenty of local trains into the Peak District of Derbyshire. I closed that invaluable railway timetable book, satisfied that all would be well with our travel arrangements.

During the evening we settled down to read through the books on Derbyshire Holmes had bought, jotting down page numbers on a slip of paper and ringing in pencil relevant points of interest we considered worthy of noting.

On exchanging books with each other, Holmes remarked how fortunate he thought we were that Mrs Hudson had chosen Derbyshire for our holiday location.

'Mind you, Watson, we must take some stout, but comfortable footwear, this appears to be hiking country *par excellence*.' The more we read about the county, the more we realised two weeks would enable us to see and visit only a fraction of what the county had to offer. This proved to be the case and the reason why the visitors we met returned year after year.

The Peak District around Bakewell appeared, we later found, to be mis-named. There were no peaks, but beautiful valleys, idyllic scenes, rugged moorlands, limestone crags and pretty villages. As Holmes was to remark, 'It truly is a landscape artist's paradise.'

We spent the next few days in preparing for our holiday. Mrs Hudson provided us with spare clean linen, whilst Holmes and I tried to pack everything we might need, from a whistle to a penknife, a sketchbook to a small brass telescope.

At last Saturday morning arrived and after an early breakfast, which Mrs Hudson insisted should be substantial, we awaited the arrival of the hansom cab we had arranged to pick us up. Before leaving, we wished the Hudsons a pleasant holiday, with Holmes reassuring them that the Baker Street Irregulars would keep a good eye on the place during our absence. Such was the holiday atmosphere amongst us that Holmes suggested we should all, as a group, have our photograph taken by a passing street photographer.

Mrs Hudson felt honoured to be in the centre of the group and said so. But Holmes, in his most expansive mood, told her that it was not only right, she being a lady, but deserved, in recognition of how well she always looked after us.

We bid our goodbyes and the hansom cab made good time because the early morning rush of traffic was over. We thus arrived at the Marylebone station early and were able to secure a first-class smoker.

With our luggage safely secured on the roof rack above our seats, Holmes took out his pipe, stoked it up, and was soon filling the air with the acrid blue smoke as he read *The Times*.

I decided to have a walk along the platform and look at the engine at the front of the train. Two small boys with their mother were there already, the boys transfixed by the maze of gleaming pipes and the glass-fronted dials in the cab.

The driver with an oil-can in his hand was climbing along the side of the boiler oiling various parts. His fireman opened the furnace door to feed it with his long-handled shovel, the heat being felt even from where we stood. The beast sizzled; the smell of hot oil was wonderful.

Wearing blue overalls and a shining black cap, the driver climbed back into the cab and, looking down from his godlike throne, invited the boys up onto the footplate. Seeing the look on the boys' faces as they were shown around reminded me of my own boyhood, when a simple gesture such as this would be remembered all one's life. They stepped down onto the platform and the driver received their thanks from mother and the boys. I hurried back to my carriage, and with a wave of the green flag from the guard the train slowly eased itself along the track. I stood by the door and lowered the window with the leather strap, waiting to see what I knew would happen; the two small boys running alongside the engine, looking with awe and admiration as the huge driving rods turned the giant driving wheels around.

Now, whether the boys distracted the driver as he eased the regulator open, I don't know, but suddenly the great wheels spun around out of control; the piston rods became for a few seconds a blur. If the wheel slip was allowed to continue, it could cause untold damage, bending the steel rods as if they were made of soft lead. The driver was quick to close the regulator, the spinning wheels slowed and the unholy noise was replaced by a steady chuff, chuff, chuff. All was well, the wheel slip was over.

I returned to my seat to find we had another passenger. He was middle aged, dressed in tweeds and appeared every inch a country gentleman; but I was wrong. He was, we were to learn, an engineer.

Holmes enjoyed listening to people; not the prattle about fashion or titillating scandal, but about the basics of life, employment, trade, science and the like. Soon the air was filled with smoke as our friend the engineer began puffing away too at his pipe, and in between puffs informed us why he was making his journey.

Holmes was content to feed him with a question now and again to keep his verbal momentum flowing. It appeared he was the director of the firm Garrett who make, amongst other things, threshing machines. Last year, he informed us, they had had a number of breakdowns with their machines.

'Now threshing time is one of the busiest times on any farm and breakdowns are drastic to the farmer, and of course to our reputation, which, I must say, is of the highest.' He puffed away and continued, 'The previous year we had redesigned a certain part of the machine and, of course, tested it to destruction, but were very concerned when we discovered it had a fault which only became evident later during the threshing season. So you see, my journey is to replace the part, which is in the guard's van, and make sure everything is in order when the threshing season begins. This is the last one we have to modify.'

He told us much interesting information about the threshing process.

We sympathised with the thought of all the hard work the farmworkers endured.

'Aye,' he remarked, 'They worked on sometimes into the dark by lantern lights to finish the work, the thresher being booked to go to another farm next day, see.'

We ate our sandwiches, exchanged and read the papers, and all in all had a most enjoyable journey. We were sorry to say goodbye to our informative and interesting engineer on changing trains at Sheffield.

Looking through the carriage window after securing seats on our train to Bakewell, I noticed on the platform among other miscellaneous goods, luggage addressed in large printing 'Leen Mills School, Hucknall, Nottinghamshire'.

I touched Holmes's knee.

'Isn't that where Lord Byron, the poet, is buried; Hucknall?'

'Yes, I believe it is, and his heart buried separately in Greece. It's said, you know, Watson, that an old prophecy foretold that when a boat should sail across Sherwood Forest full of green, then the Byron family would be no more.

'It happened, so the legend goes, a wicked member of the family had a boat made so he could sail it on the abbey lake, the same lake he had drowned his butler in. The forest people so hated the family, they threw bracken into the open boat as it journeyed through the forest, hoping to make the prophecy come true, and it did of course, the family is no more.'

'So there could be a grain of truth in prophecy after all.'

'Ah! Yes, Watson, and I prophesy the train will leave on time. The doors are crashing to, the green flag is raised and the whistle blown . . . and away we go.'

Holmes was certainly in a humorous mood. The corridor door slid open and a very overweight gentleman in a loud checked suit and bowler hat, like a racecourse bookie, slumped down into a corner seat and, after acknowledging our presence, closed his eyes.

As the train snaked its way over a multitude of points and crossovers, we were made aware of line-side factories and workshops producing the world-renowned Sheffield knives, forks, spoons and scissors. The huge satanic works and furnaces rose high, dwarfing everything around them. This was the life-blood, not only of Sheffield, but of England too. Dirty, grimy, black and likened to Bedlam, but without it where should we be?

Looking still at the passing kaleidoscope, the scene changed; mean little terraced houses gave way on the outskirts to better and even grand houses.

Yet it was strange, only minutes after changing trains and on our way into Derbyshire, we were travelling through isolated moors where the only visible form of life appeared to be sheep and the odd carrion crow. Strange indeed that in the valley where the River Don now flowed sluggish and dirty, a huge city should have arisen. Blast furnaces lit the sky at night, smoke blotted out the sun, noise shattered the air and it was here that thousands of people sweated and lived out their short lives. Yet out on the moors only the click, click, click of the rail joints reminded us, it was those same rolling mills that made the rails which bore us swiftly on our way.

The rest of the train journey to Bakewell was uneventful, except for the stout gentleman who snored loudly all the way. On arriving we booked into the Rutland Arms, before stretching our legs, looking around the old market town and walking by the river. We purchased a bakewell tart from the famous shop, shared the crumbs with a cheeky pied wagtail, and sat on a riverside seat watching a couple of anglers over the far side near the bridge, fishing for brown trout.

The little town had been busy, but nothing like the hectic crowded streets of London. The stallholders, mainly farmers' wives and daughters, were packing up their unsold eggs, cheeses and vegetables. An unsold live fowl in a cage lived to roost another night. Slowly we ambled back to our hotel, where we washed and changed.

Dinner consisted of vegetable soup, beef, boiled potatoes, vegetables and slices of a sort of heavy suet roll. It was rounded off with a cold summer pudding and coffee. In spite of the warm evening, we found it a most satisfying meal.

After the long but enjoyable day we slept well, sleeping until I was woken by a chambermaid knocking on Holmes's door to rouse him. 'Mr Holmes, sir, it's eight o'clock.' I called out that I was already awake before she tapped on my own.

We breakfasted early, and afterwards joined the Sunday morning church worshippers. The congregation comprised local gentry, farmers, tradespeople, shop-keepers and farm labourers, their wives and children. The farm labourers had had their weekly shave and looked uncomfortable in their Sunday-best clothes. All the children wore neat clean attire and needed no reminders to behave. They would rather have died than have drawn attention to themselves.

We sat at the back and drew some

furtive glances from the regular worshippers nearby. It was a joy to sing so many of the old hymns, even Holmes singing with gusto.

As the congregation filed out, we were given a further glance. We decided to stay awhile and look around the church for a few minutes, remaining unnoticed as the vicar and one of his sidesmen came back inside, down the aisle and into the vestry.

Deciding to leave without verbally agreeing, telepathic communication I suppose, we quietly passed the half-closed vestry door and heard the vicar remark, 'I was speaking to the Reverend Stevens a few days ago and he mentioned the case of the Tick Tock Man . . . he told me the village people are adamant, even if the police are not . . . that it is murder . . . However, let us get on with counting the collection, shall we?'

We almost tiptoed out of the church.

'Most interesting, Watson.'

'Very, Holmes.'

The rest of the day we spent lazily wandering around the town and surrounding walks. Both during the afternoon and evening, we came across families walking to attend church or chapel and observed that it is usual in the country to attend at least one act of worship once, most twice, and chapel folk sometimes thrice, on a Sunday.

The hotel was able to arrange transport for us in the morning to Tideswell, a large-sized village within easy reach of some spectacular walks. After a further good night's sleep, which Holmes attributed to the good country air, and before the sun had warmed the day, we and our luggage were making our way by pony and trap to Tideswell.

The driver was a cheerful young man who seemed to be acknowledged by everyone, waving and passing the time of day to various shopkeepers who were just opening their doors for the day's business.

The town was soon left behind and we were to enjoy the unspoilt countryside as, at each turn of the road, views of woods, dells and crags appeared. The driver drew to the side of the road as a flock of sheep flowed past. The shepherd said something to his dog, which immediately jumped over the wall, ran along behind it and back over again, now standing in front of the sheep, preventing them going any further. The sheep soon took advantage of the situation to crop the lush roadside herbage.

Our driver discussed something with the shepherd for a minute or so about a country matter, and then with a word to the dog from the shepherd, the sheep moved on and we were once again on our way.

Holmes remarked to the driver how the fields around Bakewell were enclosed by wooden fences, yet here the fields were divided by walls of stone. 'Ah! Well, sirs,' the driver replied, 'round Bakewell it's different land; there ain't no stones to talk of. Now up 'ere there's plenty, and stone costs nowt. The farmers clears them from the fields an' wallers just builds walls with 'em.'

'Without mortar?' queried Holmes.

'Aye, without mortar . . . in a minute just round this next turn of road, you'll find ol' Tom Jackson building one.' A few minutes later the waller could be seen in the distance, sorting out a suitable piece of stone to place in the wall.

Drawing to a halt, it was fascinating to learn how, when building a wall, first a shallow trench was dug. Large stones were then laid in it, and the wall built up gradually, with each stone carefully selected and placed so as to sit nicely on another. Small pieces of stone were used to fill in any gaps. It was a slow craftsmanlike job, but would stand for a hundred years or more.

The old waller laughed, his brown wrinkled face a picture of a contented man. 'Aye, I'll 'ave been planted many a long year afore this falls down' and he pointed to our young driver, 'an' thee an' all, young Jim.'

Arriving at Tideswell, we found it to be a large village with a wide main street and lots of cottages and houses built in random fashion off it. A small stream trickled around some of the cottages, a water vole swimming and nearby a blackbird bathing and splashing, added to the peaceful scene.

The George Hotel was large and was an ideal base for providing good clean beds, first-class meals and good ale. The landlord was most particular about his cellar, and volunteered a village worthy.

The rest of the day was spent walking around the village and surroundings.

'We mustn't overdo the walking, you know, Watson; we don't want that leg of yours playing you up.' This was true, but I couldn't help feeling Holmes, although fit and a boxer to boot, was aware that walking up hills and down again placed unusual strain on the leg muscles, not only mine, but his own.

In the evening after dinner we walked out of the hotel and into the churchyard next door. Above us screamed black swifts eager to collect the insects of the air for their hungry nestlings. The church was large and had many old gravestones dating back many years. Coming towards us along the path was a lady, with whom we passed the time of the day. She was dressed in good clothes and was obviously a person of means; the gold rings on her fingers and the pearls around her neck gave every indication of this. During our conversation she said, 'I try to put flowers every week over the children's graves.' Our questioning looks elicited from her an explanation.

'You see the mills around here, at Cromford, Carver and the rest, used to employ the orphan children from London and, I suppose, other large cities. They were brought here to the mills and terribly used, beatings and worse. They worked from early morn to late, cleaning under moving machinery the cotton dross. No wonder there were so many accidents. They wore clothes little more than rags, feeding on the poorest of food, sleeping crowded together, poor mites; although I suppose this did help keep them warm during the cold winter months.' She continued, as though driven to unburden herself.

'When they died, as so many did, some of the poor little things were brought here to be buried in unmarked pauper graves. But I know where they are buried . . . you see my great great grandfather was a mill owner.' She looked at us through tearful eyes. 'I bring flowers to put on those little children's graves . . . I can give charity to the living, but I can do nothing for those poor dead children. I try to think it helps in some small way to make amends for my family's misdeeds.' She turned away without another word, dabbing the tears from her eyes.

We watched her walk out of the gates. 'The human soul has infinite facets, Watson. But to bear the guilt of our forebears is one I have never encountered before. Now I understand what prompted the words, 'those dark satanic mills'.'

' 'And did those feet in ancient times, walk upon England's mountains green'.'

'Exactly, Watson.'

We returned to the George for a nightcap before retiring, nothing how, as we walked out into the street, small bats flittered around now, replacing the daytime hunting swifts.

The following morning we set out to begin our holiday proper. Dressed in breeches, stout boots and carrying knapsacks containing maps, compass and telescope, to name just a few of the items we felt we might need, we set forth. Climbing up hill and down dale, we realised why the Peak District is called England's Switzerland.

Resting at times just to admire the views and at others to watch and listen to birds like the nuthatch, chiff-chaff, jay and both the green and the great-spotted woodpeckers, we walked in a different world, a world we had forgotten existed.

Holmes took out his gold hunter. 'It's after eleven, I fancy, Watson we should head for this village 'Nether Froggatt' here.' He pointed to it on the map. A quick calculation made it less than three miles away. Three miles on pavements can be walked in less than an hour easily, but along narrow wooded paths, up hill and down, took considerably longer.

Pleased at last to arrive, we sought out the one and only place in the village where we could rest outside, obtain a drink and eat our sandwiches. It was hardly an inn, but the ale was cool and thirst quenching. We ordered a second round in quick time congratulating the landlord on his brew.

The sandwiches the George Hotel had packed up for us were good, and we enjoyed sitting outside in the sunshine just resting. Nothing stirred, a more peaceful place would have been hard to find.

'Tick tock, tick tock, tick tock. Kiefernzapfen, kiefernzapfen, kiefernzapfen.' The voice was clear, loud and unmistakable. The last words were guttural, haunting and spine chilling. We listened without moving, then slowly turned and looked at each other.

'Tick tock, tick tock, tick tock. Kiefernzapfen, kiefernzapfen, kiefernzapfen.' The last words again ending in that same horrible haunting spine-chilling sound. Clearly, loudly, it was repeated over and over again. Slowly, Holmes and I stood up, turned around and walked backwards, whilst at the same time looking upwards to the roof of the inn.

'Tick tock, tick tock, tick tock. Kiefernzapfen, kiefernzapfen, kiefernzapfen.' There perched on the ridge tiles we were astonished to see a huge bird. This was no ordinary bird, but a huge raven. The iridescent beauty of its midnight plumage of purple, blue and green gloss, was breathtaking. A formidable beak, massive and hooked, opened and closed as it continued its litany of tick tock, tick tock, tick tock. Kiefernzapfen, kiefernzapfen, kiefernzapfen.

'It's a raven, isn't it, Holmes?' I whispered.

He replied in like subdued tones. 'Yes, one of the largest of the corvid tribe, has a wingspan of some four feet, and in flight is among our most skilled acrobatic birds.'

The raven ceased its mimicry and preened itself. In a low voice Holmes continued, 'It was once a common bird, but since the gentry's gamekeepers have shot every other creature that might threaten their pheasants, their decline has been rapid.

'Gamekeepers are the enemy of every other creature that walks or flies, excepting of course, their masters' sacrificial pheasants, poor things, cosseted to die in a hail of lead shot.'

'True, Holmes. I remember one game-keeper who shot all the nightingales on his preserve, believing they kept his pheasants awake at night. On his gibbet he had cats, badgers, foxes, buzzards, hawks and owls, but no ravens, they were already rare by then.'

'Quite right, sir.' We turned to see the landlord standing in the doorway. 'When I wore a lad, they wore seen around a lot, but you don't see 'em any more.'

'Except now . . . here,' retorted Holmes.

I said, 'But why this strange mimicry of a ticking clock ending with those horrible frightful guttural words . . . and where has it come from?' The landlord came and sat on an empty barrel.

'It's a bit of a mystery really, gentlemen. Many years ago some children found it and thought it was a young jackdaw. When it wore discovered like, that it wore a raven, nobody wanted it. Ravens, you know, are supposed to be connected wi' death, an' they thought it might bring bad luck to the family.'

Just then the raven gave a few more

157

tick tocks and flew off crying out in a harsh voice, 'Kwark, kwark, kwark,' the raven's natural cry finishing off with what could only be described as foreign guttural words, screaming those same words over and over again as it flew to another part of the village.

Holmes whipped out his notebook, quickly wrote something, then snapped it shut.

The landlord continued, 'I suppose the superstition is true, 'cause the owd clockmaker, the Tick Tock Man who kept 'im as a pet, died three weeks ago. He wore found dead in 'is chair, the door open, the place in disarray, an' the raven gone. The folks around 'ere reckon there wore more to his death though, not natural like.'

Just then a shout calling him, came from inside the inn. 'I'll 'ave to go; wife's dad wants 'elp getting up to privy.'

A villager opposite the inn came to his cottage door and scraped the remains on his plate, onto the ground. The raven, which must now have returned and was close by, flew down, picked up the largest morsel and flew off with it.

We should have liked to have heard more from the landlord, but decided not to wait, and instead looked around the nearby church. 'I always think of churchyards as a record written on stone, of the past, you know, Watson.'

I agreed. 'Look at that headstone, nearly a hundred and eighty years old. Each generation adding their names, right up to the present decade.'

'Each generation most likely being born, living and dying here. Incredible to believe that most never even went further than a few miles outside the village boundary. And those that did probably only ventured as far as the next village. But the bicycle will change all that, Watson.'

'Do you think it will?'

Holmes stopped in his stride. 'The invention of the bicycle will change the way we live. It will enable ordinary people, those that can afford one, of course, to bicycle, five, ten times the distance they could have hoped to have walked. Work and jobs within ten or fifteen miles will be possible to travel to.'

At that moment who should be observed leaving the rectory and heading towards us was none other than the vicar. Holmes remarked, 'I see the vicar has noticed our presence and is anxious to exchange a bit of conversation with strangers, as a change from the local worthies, no doubt.'

As usual, Holmes was quite correct in his assumption. The vicar smiled and shook hands with us both, introducing himself as the Reverend Stevens. Holmes introduced me as Mr Moxon and himself as Soames. I never questioned this by even batting an eyelid, but assumed he had good reason.

The vicar was eager to show us around the church and was a most pleasant, affable man. The inside of the church was cool and most welcome as a place to escape from the heat of the afternoon. After giving us a most interesting account of the church's history, he took us out through the vestry and into the churchyard.

Following him, we came upon a recent burial site. The grass sods upon it were uneven with the edges turning brown from the heat of the sun. A simple jamjar halfburied at the head of the grave held some fresh wild flowers. The vicar indicating the flowers said, 'The children put them there . . . called him the Tock Tock Man. They used to love to see the clocks ticking away on his workshop wall, and of course, the cuckoo clocks were a great novelty. He spoke with a foreign accent and the children thought this funny, but he didn't mind. They found him kind and miss him very much.'

'Yes,' said Holmes. 'He was German, wasn't he?'

Both the vicar and I stopped and stared at him. 'Yes, he was.' The vicar paused. 'Did you know him?'

'Oh, no! I think the landlord mentioned it.' I knew this to be untrue, but said nothing. The vicar looked up at the church clock which began to strike the hour of three. 'Look, would you do me the honour of having afternoon tea with me? I'm afraid it will only be cake and scones, as my good wife is out visiting a sick woman in the village.'

Holmes responded, 'I assure you, the honour is ours and cake and scones will be more than adequate.'

We followed him out of the churchyard, through a small gate and into the grounds of the rectory. A swing was tied up and a rabbit hutch empty, giving evidence that the vicar's children had grown up, were at college, university, or making their own way in the world.

A cook answered the bell, still wiping her wet hands on her apron. A few whispered words and he replied, 'Cake and scones will be fine. I know the mistress has taken the ham with her.' She withdrew from the large cool drawing-room.

I was surprised to observe all the walls were covered with tapestries from ceiling to floor. In winter no doubt, making the room snug and warm and in summer cool. 'What a sensible idea we have let go out of fashion,' I remarked.

Our conversation went back and forth,

the vicar obviously greatly interested in our London gossip, and the description we gave him of the political scene, especially when we dropped prominent names. This wasn't to impress him with the reflected glory it gave us, but we felt it was a reward for his kindness. It would give endless pleasure in the weeks ahead when, for the umpteenth time, he would recount how the two gentlemen from London, had spoken of Lord So-and-So, and Mr So-and-So of the Home Office, and lots of other important people.

It was after a little rosy-cheeked maid had brought in a further pot of hot water that Holmes remarked, 'Whilst we were refreshing ourselves at lunchtime with a glass of the landlord's excellent brew, we were entertained by the now departed clockmaker's raven.'

The vicar smiled, 'You were, were you? Yes, it's a remarkable bird, reared it from a squab he did. The village boys thought it was a young jackdaw, but when Jimmy Fletcher's mother discovered it was a raven, a harbinger of death they believe, she told him to get rid of it. Of course the mothers of all the other children would not have it either.' He offered us another scone, but we declined.

'Well, the Tick Tock Man felt sorry for the poor thing, neglected and starving. It opened its beak to every passing villager, begging for food. No one would take it for fear of the reputation ravens have, being afraid it might invite death into the family if they harmed it. There is an old myth you know among country people, that if its cry is heard near a sick person, for instance, then death would soon follow. Its awesome sepulchral eerie cry, of course, add to its macabre reputation.'

Holmes finished the story, 'So the Tick Tock Man took it in and it became his pet, and a mimic into the bargain.'

I put my tea cup down. 'Until I heard the raven mimic the sound of a ticking clock, I had no idea they were mimics. Jackdaws, magpies and starlings, yes, but not ravens.'

Holmes replied, 'It is not common knowledge, but ravens are among the best mimics in the avian world, and with it is said, some understanding. While in the case of the parrot, it is rare that it advances beyond a few set phrases.'

The vicar made a point, 'Few people realise that the parrot was with us in the Dark Ages. Priests used them to delude the weak and superstitious minds of the people. One cardinal it is reputed, paid a hundred gold pieces, an astronomical fortune in those days, for a parrot that could, without pause or hesitation, repeat the whole of the Apostle's Creed.'

'Most interesting,' replied Holmes. 'It is without doubt, the sailor, who on his long sea journeys taught the young parrots, bought for pence in faraway ports, to talk and made them so popular. It earned Jack Tar extra funds to swell his drinking money upon reaching his home port.' Holmes nodded across to me, 'I think I remember you once retailing to me a very interesting story about a parrot, Moxon.'

'Quite right, Soames,' said I, enjoying using his new name. 'It concerned a parrot who was kept outside a quayside public house, in good weather of course. Now this parrot picked up the lingo of the drivers giving orders to their horses when positioning them, loading or unloading cargo.

'One day a horse and cart were left unattended near the water's edge, and were spied by the mischievous parrot, who mimicked the gruff voice of a driver, 'Wo! back, back, Whoa!, back, back, back.' The unsuspicious horse obliged and obliged time after time, as the delighted bird repeated the command, till horse and cart tipped over the edge of the harbour, and the poor animal was drowned.' Both Holmes and the vicar expressed admiration for the account, but we all felt sorry for the horse.

The vicar asked if we wished for further tea and obliged us, the little maid bringing in more hot water. Sitting down again he regaled us with a further anecdote about the ways of the parrot family.

'This story was told to me by a parishioner who had lived most of his life in London, but on retiring and being a widower, came to live with his sister. I have no doubt the story is true; the teller was not one to invent or exaggerate. He had kept a shop opposite the inn where the incident happened.

'The parrot in question was kept by the inn-keeper to amuse his patrons and was a capital talker. Everyone knew the parrot in Kensington because its cage was hung out of an upper window and it would amuse itself from morning to night chattering away hailing every fruit-vendor and itinerant merchant who passed below.

'One day a highly respectable old gentleman in brown gaiters, top hat and carrying an umbrella was stopped in his tracks as the parrot, in a state of high hilarity, screamed out at the top of its voice, 'Cod, oh! cod oh! plaice and eels alive oh!' He peered up, as the parrot in a highly excited state still repeated over and over again the cry 'Cod, oh! cod oh! plaice and eels alive oh!' causing the old gentleman to lean against the wall, and laugh until the tears rolled down his cheeks. The reason for his hilarity was explained to the gathering crowd, when he related that the bird must have the memory of a tax collector. He remembers me, despite my fine clothes. Twenty years ago he told the crowd, when I was a poor struggling fishmonger, I drove my fish cart every day along this street calling out, 'Cod, oh! cod, oh! plaice and eels alive oh!' Admonishing the bird with a wagging finger, he warned, 'I mustn't come through Kensington again if I wish to forget I was once a poor fishmonger'.'

We all laughed, even the little housemaid tittered, whom I observed listening behind the open drawing-room door.

Although we all found the subject of mimicry fascinating, Holmes decided to change the subject when he remarked:

'I understand from the landlord, that the old clockmaker was found dead in his chair, and the door open, through which the raven escaped.'

The vicar looked slightly uneasy when he replied, 'Yes, that is true, but to say the raven escaped is incorrect. You see, it had been his companion and pet for many, many years. It was like a dog or cat, it came and went whenever it

168

pleased, flying all over the village, a regular sight. It would perch by the clockmaker's chair and there they would sit together by the fireside, like true companions.

'It was the frantic unusual behaviour of the raven that caused the village folk to suspect there was something amiss. The bird appeared agitated and flew about the village, seeming not to settle for any length of time in any one place. Instead of its usual mimicry of tick tock, tick tock, it screamed them aloud in a most dreadful way, but now ended with the same foreign word kiefernzapfen, repeating it over and over again. The whole village was mystified. On investigation, they found the old clockmaker was dead.'

Holmes surprised me by bluntly stating, 'But the villagers suspect it was an unnatural death. What reason leads them to think so, not just the bird's unusual behaviour surely?'

The vicar was taken aback, not sure how to reply, but decided it was better to admit his fears, perhaps beginning to suspect we were plain-clothes policemen.

'You are quite correct. My friend, Dr Draycott from Bakewell, examined him and found a wound above his right ear. There was blood from it all over his right shoulder and neck. However, according to him, it would not have been of sufficient injury to have caused his death. Dr Draycott considered he may have died from heart failure.'

He said no more, wondering no doubt if we would be satisfied with the amount of information he had disclosed. Holmes was not, and gently prodded him further.

'What else besides the wound, and the blood, makes them uneasy about his death?'

I think the vicar now felt it was useless to withhold any information further, despite he and the doctor having agreed to keep their fears to themselves. They both apparently felt nothing would be served by upsetting the villagers with suspicions of a murder having been committed, without more real evidence.

'You ask what else made them uneasy? Well, there were several drawers in his

170

sideboard pulled out as though they had been searched, a stool and the raven's perch were knocked over, the whole room was in disarray, and of course, the door was left wide open.' He paused for a few moments, 'I should tell you too, the clockmaker had always said that when he died, everything he owned would be left in trust to build a row of almshouses for the poor. Any money left over, should be used to keep them in good repair. This, of course, was common knowledge in the village.

'Although he lived a rather frugal life and to the casual observer appeared as if he was worth nothing, I always suspected he had money hidden away . . . '

'Why?' asked Holmes with a questioning look.

The vicar appeared rather uneasy, but continued.

'I understand it is common to bury or hide wealth in Europe. Invading armies would plunder and pass on. When a war was over, the wealth would be unearthed again. He was, as you said, German. I think he buried or hid his money, using this old and tried habit, rather than a bank.'

'Do you know anything more about him?' asked Holmes. I was sure now the vicar suspected we were police. Holmes's form of questioning went beyond ordinary casual interest.

'His name was Hans Reitsch and he was middle aged when he arrived here thirty-odd years ago. Why he came here to this particular village we never knew. It was many, many years before his English was sufficiently good enough to hold a conversation with him, and by that time, the villagers had lost their curiosity and just accepted him as a nice old man with a foreign accent.'

Holmes pressed on, terse and to the point. 'So you are saying, you and the doctor found no money in the cottage?'

'That is so. We searched the cottage thoroughly both before and after the old man was buried, but found nothing . . . ' He paused, then uneasily I thought, continued, 'I am not happy to disclose this, because it is casting a shadow of suspicion on a man who could be perfectly innocent, but I would be failing in my duty if I withheld this additional information. A gypsy family stayed for several weeks on the outskirts of the village, making pegs and weaving baskets. They moved on a few days before the old clockmaker died. Now, one of the gypsies was seen leaving the clockmaker's cottage with a clock under his arm, a day or so before they upped and left. So you see, he would have talked with the clockmaker and would know the layout of the cottage. There, then, is the sum total of my suspicions, and I must stress, that is all they are, suspicions.'

Before either Holmes or I could reply to his disclosures, he looked at us both in turn and said, 'Talking of suspicions . . . my own are that you two gentlemen are not ramblers on holiday, but policemen?'

Holmes spoke out in a clear, precise, but friendly voice. 'I feel we should offer you an apology . . . we are not policemen, we are private detectives. We work for the government from time to time.' Holmes and I exchanged significant glances. 'We hold no official position and as such are free of restraints which exist in the constabulary . . . and of course, vice versa, the government are free of any embarrassment connecting us with Whitehall, should we . . . what shall I say . . . slip up.' He laughed and continued, 'It is said that fact is stranger than fiction . . . we are in fact, on holiday away from our London office, and really are rambling, enjoying the wonderful scenery of your county.'

The vicar looked less apprehensive as Holmes continued, 'Unlike the old clockmaker, we can tell you why and how we came to be in your village.' He then recounted how we had chosen to ramble Derbyshire, and the Peak District in particular, from all the many other lovely locations in Britain. 'So you see, sir, that like your good self, who is never off duty when he sees the Lord's good work to be done, so it is with we detectives. We can smell out a case, yes even in the air made sweet from the fields full of your wild summer flowers.'

The vicar was now placated by Holmes's

unusual but friendly explanation. However, I failed yet to see why Holmes introduced us as Soames and Moxon . . . in time I knew all would be revealed. Holmes quickly rose to his feet, I more slowly.

'Just one more point, sir. I presume the watchmaker relied upon the trade brought in by carriers from nearby villages?'

The vicar placed his hands together as though in prayer. 'That is correct. The carriers would bring them in and later, when repaired, return them. He never charged anything like the prices they would have paid in Bakewell or Baslow. This, of course, endeared him to the village folk. And, of course, when he had no repairs to carry out, he made the movements of clocks for several Cabinet makers in the area who in turn, when they too had no orders, made long-case clocks.'

'Now, sir, could we impose upon your time and generosity just a little more, to ask if we may be allowed to look over the cottage, accompanied of course by your good self. Perhaps the middle of tomorrow morning?' The vicar's face showed relief and even pleasure at our proposed visit. His friend, the good Dr Draycott, could hardly object considering our connections with the seat of government administration, Whitehall.

However, owing to a previous appointment on the morrow, we had to arrange our inspection for the following day. After shaking hands and thanking the vicar for his hospitality, we made our way back to Tideswell.

There was little conversation between us as we made our way back. I think each of us was turning over in our minds the conversation we had had with the vicar. And then, of course, there was the strange behaviour of the raven.

We had made the mistake of misjudging the distance we had walked in the morning, each mile now seemed longer than the last. Needless to say, it gave us an enormous appetite. We were ravenous and ate all that was set before us, fried sweetbreads with vegetables followed by stewed rhubarb with arrowroot custard, stilton, port and coffee. After this a turn around the village we felt was called for, it being still daylight of course.

Outside a bow-fronted shop selling new and secondhand books, a young man was unloading stock from a dogcart, and obligingly let us meander around, whilst he continued to unload.

With an eye to my possible future needs, I bought a book titled 'Small Business Accounting Made Easy'. Holmes, I noticed, engrossed himself all the time in one book, German/English translation, but did not purchase it, instead buying a tatty book from the 'Bargain Shelf' without even opening it, as a means of patronage.

We arranged through the offices of mine host at the George to hire the same trap and driver to take us on the morrow to the village of Eyam, the plague village. We were determined not to make our holiday into a marathon hike, so travelling by horse and trap saved a lot of walking time which we used to better advantage, stopping, admiring the views, talking to the locals, and generally making our holiday an enjoyable occasion.

The trap next morning was on time,

driven by Jim, who we learned later, was the son of a local stone mason. Stone and stone masonry is a big trade and industry in Derbyshire. He added to what he had already told us yesterday, about stone being found, only a few inches in some places, below the surface of the soil. This was confirmed by the outcrops we saw by the roadside; most of the dividing walls having been built of it. We were both educated and entertained by our young driver, and encouraged the young lad to chatter away, learning much of the local history and about the lovely village we were to visit.

It transpired that in 1665, when London was devastated by the worst plague ever, a stage coach from the city delivered a box of clothes to a journeyman tailor, called George Viccars, who lived in the village.

There must have been a flea, which carried the plague germ, among the musty damp clothes, because within four days the poor man was dead. No one of course realised that fleas carried the plague.

' 'Tis said, sirs, that afore winter twenty-three more tipped up their toes an' died,' Jim informed us.

We drew into the side of the narrow road to allow four huge shire horses pulling a heavy load of limestone to rumble by. 'That's stone for a big new house; 'tis being built in Tideswell. It's a growing village is Tideswell; they calls the church you knows the cathedral of the Peak, 'cos it's so big.' He shook the reins and we moved off again into the middle of the road at a smart pace. The roads were kept in reasonable repair by roadmen. We came upon one outside his cottage, sitting on a low stool, breaking stones into small pieces with a hammer. His donkey was nearby, cropping the lush grass. The lad stopped and had a word with him. The roadman got up and went inside his cottage, to return a few moments later with a dead rabbit. The lad took it and dropped it on the floor, between Holmes and me. The roadman grinned, a missing front tooth giving him a jovial expression. 'He's a big buck, but young, shud mek a reet good dinner.'

The lad thanked him and we continued on our journey.

I wanted to keep the lad talking, wanting to learn more about their way of life in the country, compared with ours in the town. Holmes always reasoned you learn more from talking to people, than from books. With people, you can obtain further information by coaxing the conversation in the right direction, but with a book, it is restricted to what is printed. A good point I suppose.

He illustrated this maxim by saying to the lad, 'I see no money exchanged hands. Was the rabbit a gift?' The lad took his eyes from the road ahead to look at Holmes and grinned. 'Sort of, more an exchange really. We country folk use barter a lot, not only wi' goods, but in doing jobs for each other like.'

'So what did you barter for the rabbit?'

'Me dad's brother lets him glean from the corn stubble after harvest. 'E gets enough corn to feed 'is 'ens through winter. So niver gus short a eggs does Joe. 'Is missis exchanges the eggs she don't need for summut from the grocer man, when he cums by every wick.'

The lad certainly educated us in the ways of how the economy in the countryside worked. Barter we knew had existed long before money. In the countryside, it still played a most useful role it seemed.

We careered down the hill at a good trot and saw spread before us the lovely old village of Eyam. The limestone cottages, their colour mellowed by centuries of the elements, were now bathed in sunshine, as tranquil a scene as one could ever wish to see. We arranged with the lad a suitable time to take us back again, before setting out on foot to explore.

The village will always be remembered for the way the god-fearing folk contained the pestilence, preventing it spreading to other nearby villages by isolating themselves. At the centre of the village, there was a bull-ring set in a block of stone in the ground. A reminder of not so many years past, when a terrified bull or bear was chained to it, and dogs were encouraged to attack the tethered

181

animal. Dogs and beast were terribly injured: blood, hair and flesh; a gory sight, all in the name of sport and as a spectacle during Wakes Week. It was declared illegal in 1835. Now all that is in the past, the bull-ring just a reminder of those bad times.

As we walked through the village, we passed the time of day with the folk we met, many of whom were sitting outside their cottages, knitting, sewing, pegging rugs, or just enjoying the warmth of the sun.

Walking the length of the village we came to a building, not much larger than a barn, which sported a painted board proclaiming it to be the 'Townhead Factory.' Upon making enquiries from a passing local, we learned of its unique history. It had been built in 1735 as a silk-weaving mill. Now, a certain Mr Ralph Wayne had discovered how to weave on both sides of the material. His silk was therefore much sought after.

However, it was the apex of the factory wall that Holmes and I found to be most interesting. There were pigeon holes leading into the loft. The pigeon holes were for carrier pigeons to take messages between the factory and the silk supplier in Macclesfield. One could not help but admire the initiative of the idea, when one considers the time it would have taken to travel the thirty or so winding miles, up hill and down dale, compared with a pigeon completing the distance in perhaps thirty minutes.

As we walked through the village, Holmes and I discussed the need for the silk supplier at Macclesfield to also have a loft of homing pigeons, to send back the reply. Pigeons only fly in one direction, that is, back to their home loft, so presumably the pigeons were returned by road carrier, when they next made a delivery, thus enabling them to be available for use next time.

We were in deep discussion about this arrangement, when we came across an open space that had once been the market of the town, because, as villages go, Eyam is large and would have been considered in times past as a small town. There still remained a village hall and a set of stocks, used no doubt in the past to punish drunkards and others for petty misdemeanours.

It was whilst we were examining them that we became aware of a gentleman bidding farewell to someone at the upstairs window of the Hall opposite. No doubt, from her appearance, she was a member of the family who lived there. Eyam Hall, we observed, was a wonderful seventeenth-century building built by the side of the road, with wide steps leading up from lawned gardens. We averted our eyes from the couple, but were pleasantly surprised when the gentleman came across to us and introduced himself as a friend of the family.

'You are ramblers, I presume, enjoying the good clean air and exercise?' We agreed we were, and that Derbyshire was a delightful country, especially for visitors like ourselves. The woods, tumbling streams and tiny hamlets were a complete contrast to London town. We said how interested we were to learn more about the plague which had been inflicted upon the village all those years ago.

Our gentleman friend was only too pleased to acquaint us with the history, he being a native of the village and a local historian.

'Well, gentlemen, as you are probably aware, it was the bubonic plague which came to England because of our trade with the Orient. The fleas carrying the bubonic plague came from the black rats, which ships carrying silk and spices brought from China. It was not very long before the plague was rampant in London. This was in the year 1665, and the rich people who could afford to leave, fled. Those who remained died in their thousands.' Holmes and I sat on a low stone wall enjoying both the sunshine and the historical account. He continued.

'Late in August of that year a parcel of clothing was delivered to one George Viccars, a local tailor from London. When he saw the cloth was damp, he put it in front of the fire to dry. Two days later he developed a fever, swellings and a rose-red rash blotched the skin. Two days later he died, the first victim in the village.'

I looked towards Holmes. This tallied word for word with Jim's account of the plague. Our historian continued with more facts.

'Two more people died and, as the disease spread, the numbers increased. The dead were buried in rough graves close to their homes, in an effort to contain the spread of the infection. One villager, a Mrs Hancock, carried out seven members of her family and buried them in the field next to her house.'

'It must have been a harrowing time for the village folk, a most frightening situation,' I commiserated.

He made a half-circle motion with his hand indicating the countryside. 'Yes, a few people packed up and fled, including the Bradshaw family from Bradshaw Hall.

'It was then the heroes of the day stepped in, the rector, William Mompesson, and his non-conformist colleague, Thomas Stanley. They implored the village people to stay inside the village boundary, and thus prevent the plague spreading to the rest of the nearby villages, and to the whole county. A most courageous plea to make of anyone.'

Just then a flock of sheep came along the road being shepherded by an old man and a couple of dogs. 'Excuse me a moment whilst I have a word with the shepherd.' The dogs kept the sheep in a huddle, nervous and apprehensive. At last, with a wave of his hand and the touch of a forelock, the two parted company, the sheep eager to move on.

'Sorry about that, but I wanted to ask about his wife, she is very ill. Where was I? Oh, yes. Rector Mompesson, with the help of the Earl of Devonshire, arranged for supplies of food, and other essentials needed by the village folk, to be left at the place called the 'boundary stone'. Money payments for these provisions were disinfected by placing the coins in running stream water, or in vinegar.' He rubbed his thigh, shook his leg and continued. 'Touch of the screws.

'The village folk, realising the seriousness of their plight, became frightened to gather together, even for Sunday worship. The rector therefore closed the church, and held open airservices instead. On August the twenty-fifth, sadly Catherine, wife of the rector, died, she being the last victim of the plague.

'The village folk had through their fortitude contained the disease, but at great cost to themselves; some two hundred and fifty-nine souls had made the sacrifice. They had shown true courage and Christianity.'

'And yet while the great plague raged throughout England,' recounted Holmes, 'Parliament still found time to pass an Act, that all shrouds must be made of wool; said to help the expansion of the wool trade.' Holmes and I were very moved by his account, thanking our historian friend for his time and information. We all shook hands.

'Look around the church, you will find it most interesting.' With a smile and a wave, he picked up his walking stick and strode away.

We did visit the church which was very close by, and found it to have been dedicated to St Lawrence, the Christian preacher, who was asked apparently to hand over the treasures of his church to the prefect of Rome. He presented his people instead. The prefect, angry at having been tricked, had Lawrence put to death by roasting him on a grid iron. 'Not a very Christian act. But then, the acts of the Spanish inquisitors were all performed in the supposed name of religion,' remarked Holmes drily.

In the north aisle of the church we discovered a cupboard reputedly made from the very box containing the plague-infested cloth, delivered to George Viccars the tailor. Poking around further, Holmes said, 'Read this, Watson . . . being a medical man this should interest you.' I went over to him and saw he had found among a dust-laden collection of ecclesiastical papers and worn-out hymn books, tattered and beyond repair, an old copy of how to cure a sore or carbuncle. It read:

Dated 1695 Remedy for Sores and Carbuncles.
Take Bay Salt, Rye Meal and Yolks of Eggs as many as will make them

into a paste; then spread it on to a piece of leather and apply it to the Sore or Carbuncle and it will draw the poison to the Centre, so that the Sore will ripen; and being broke, the infection will come away; to expedite the Cure of which, when it is broke, put the Rump of a live chicken to the mouth of the sore, so that its vent may be placed on it, and will draw the infection into the body of the Chicken, in so much that it will dye, and so will one or two more if the infection be great; but when they cease to do so, it is a sign that the Poison is exhausted, and the party in a very fair way of recovering Health.

Another remedy, this time prescribed by the College of Physicians, no less:

Take a great Onion, hollow it, put into it a fig, rue cut small, and a dram of Venice treacle; put it close stopt into wet paper and roast it in the embers; apply it hot to the tumour; lay three or four, one after the other; let one lie three hours.

'Most interesting, Holmes. I might be tempted to try it on some awkward recalcitrant patient when next I locum.'

Holmes chuckled. 'If you do, I want to come and see you do it.'

I copied down the cure in my notebook for future reference. Wandering still around the church we came across the actual chair in which the Reverend Mompesson had sat. It was of good English oak with the legs firmly held by stretchers. Carved with the date 1665, it appeared good for many a hundred years to come. We could have stayed much longer absorbing the history of the lovely old church, but tore ourselves away reluctantly, and went out into the street, momentarily blinded by the bright sunlight.

Walking along we passed the actual cottage where George Viccars the tailor lodged, and from where the outbreak of the plague began.

'See, Watson, nothing has changed, the

same worn doorstep as Viccars trod, the same small windows he must have looked through, when the stage-coach delivered him his box of death. Yet over two hundred and thirty years have passed; truly these villages are timeless.'

We ate at the Miners' Arms Inn where we were informed, when talking with the landlord, that a certain Reverend Joseph Hunt was involved in a mock marriage performed at the inn in 1683. Whether officiating or his own, the landlord was unable to say. Having drunk two pints of his good ale and eaten our beef sandwiches, we shouldered our rucksacks and ambled forth.

Following the landlord's instructions we found yet another reminder of the plague, Merrill House. The owner, Humphrey Merrill, left the house during the plague to live in a hut in isolation out on the moor, and thus survived.

It was later in the afternoon, just walking along, when Holmes suddenly tugged my sleeve, and pointed to an encampment some distance away. 'I think the gathering fits the description the vicar gave us, bell tent and all. The raggle-taggle-gypsies, oh!'

I looked, and in a clearing I could see a gypsy caravan. Not the lovely shaped ornate kind with decorations of swirls and gold leaf, but a plain box affair, akin to the type seen behind a steam-roller. It was constructed of vertical planks, and in need of a good paint. Beside it was erected an old tatty bell tent used, no doubt, to work in during inclement weather. A couple of lurcher dogs and several children ran around the site.

'Can you feign a limp, Watson?' I gave him a blank look, cudgelling my brain.

'Perhaps not . . . put a pebble in your boot. You are going to limp over to the gypsies and ask if they have a bowl of water to soak your sprained ankle in.'

I still could not understand what Holmes had in mind; realising this, he explained further.

'It is a ploy, Watson. We ask for their help putting them in a dominant position and, hopefully, allaying any suspicion. It will give us an excuse to speak with them.'

I now saw it all, and duly obliged. The pebble in my boot made it impossible to forget to limp, even for one moment. 'And another thing, Watson, we must approach the site not from this direction, but from over there. We would hardly have limped through the village without taking advantage of the opportunity to get help from some cottager.'

As we approached the camp, the children stopped their play, and the dogs barked. On arriving, two women came to the door of the caravan and down the steps. They both wore blouses and dark skirts, their shining black hair tied in a bun.

Holmes introduced ourselves. 'I wonder if we could elicit your help . . . my friend here has sprained his ankle, and we hoped you had a bowl of water in which he could bathe it?' The young woman remained silent, but the older one smiled and nodded her head. 'Certainly, sir, I will get you a stool each to sit on.'

She spoke to the silent shy children and there was a rush into the tent to fetch them. I can't remember all the conversation, as I was busy taking off my boot and sock, easing my foot into the cold water. But Holmes seemed to have charmed the women, even the young one smiled and flashed her large dark eyes at him. I heard her reply to Holmes, 'Oh, we get by. The men are away cutting wood for the pegs just now.'

'You know, it's wonderful how you make these pegs out of . . . nothing really,' said Holmes, picking up a clothes peg from a nearby basket full of them. The younger woman threw back her head and laughed with a touch of scorn I thought. 'Hardly nothing. We choose the wood; it has to be supple, scrounge the tins and cut them into thin strips.' She looked proud, her figure slim and lithe, going on to explain, 'We bind the top of the peg with the thin strip of tin, like this, and tack through it like so.' Wielding a small hammer, she drove the tack through the tin and into the wood with one swift blow. Then taking hold of a knife, she held the peg and pressing downwards against the top of a barrel, made a cut. The clothes peg was finished. Free wood, scrounged tin and a tack became a peg.

Holmes took the peg from her and examined it. 'As I said, hardly nothing, but a lot of skill involved.' He turned to me, 'Is it feeling any easier, Watson?'

'Yes, Holmes, in fact the water feels so good I'm going to put my other foot in too.' So saying I unlaced my other boot, took off my sock and immersed it.

Holmes addressed the younger woman. 'You wouldn't happen to know the time, would you? My friend here forgot his watch in the rush to pack for our holiday, and I had the misfortune to drop mine. It hasn't gone since.' I nodded agreement, guessing the ploy.

The older woman was busy taking down some of the dried washing off the clothes line. The children sat, wide eyed and fascinated by their unusual visitors. The young woman replied:

'Of course I can tell you the time, sir; my husband got our clock repaired only a few weeks ago when we were camped outside Nether Froggatt.' She looked inside the caravan and came back down the steps. 'It's nearly four o'clock. Ours had broken its spring, but it's all right now. The old clockmaker made a good job of repairing it . . . he was a lovely man, my husband said, lived in a cottage with a raven for company of all things. Wouldn't take a penny for repairing it either. When he learned we had three children, he gave my husband a sixpence to share between them. If you are walking near there, it would be worth your while to see if he could repair it.'

'I'll try to put my boot on, Holmes. It feels much better now.' So saying, I dried my feet on a small hand towel from my rucksack and put my socks and boots back on, not forgetting to drop a pebble in one of them to make me limp away.

We thanked the gypsies who refused our offered money, insisting it was the least they could do to help a fellow traveller. As we passed the children, still sitting on the ground, Holmes whispered into the ear of each one and slipped something under each little round bottom.

As I limped away, Holmes hissed,

'You're limping with the wrong foot.'

I replied in some agitation, 'I know, but I only realised my mistake when I stood up to move off . . . perhaps they won't notice. By the way, Holmes, what did you whisper to the children?'

Holmes turned around and waved to them. 'I told them to sit tight until we were out of sight and then discover what they were sitting upon.'

'And what are they sitting upon?'

'A florin each, Watson,' and with that we turned around once more to wave our last farewells, the children waving back, wide eyed and smiling until we were out of sight.

I quickly found somewhere to sit and removed the offending pebble.

'Well, Watson, we can discount the gypsies as having anything to do with the old watchmaker's death . . . agreed?'

'Absolutely. Ah! That's better,' as I stood up and made a few short strides.

' 'Pon my word,' remarked Holmes, 'I was impressed by the women's speech. Each spoke well, but moving around the countryside, and never staying long enough to be influenced by any local dialect, may be the reason.' I agreed and could not help thinking that in any situation, these women were more than capable of holding their own. The young one certainly impressed Holmes, I could tell. As we walked along, I pondered on the way Holmes had obtained his information, admiring the simple ploy which had achieved a perfect result.

Our faithful Jim was waiting for us at the appointed time and place to take us back to the George, tired but pleasantly so.

It was later that evening when I thought to ask Holmes why he had become Soames and I, Moxon. He puffed at his pipe and leaned back against the rough wood of the garden seat we both sat on. Above us the swifts kept up their wheeling and diving, in a constant search of the skies for insects.

'As I see it, Watson, we are on holiday and if we are to benefit from it, we must be seen as just two gentlemen taking a rambling holiday. Yet when we spoke to the vicar yesterday, I felt he was uneasy about something, and out of habit, fell into my line of questioning, which I admit went beyond ordinary casual interest, so much so, he suspected we were policemen, correct?' I nodded. 'I didn't want to reveal our true identities, so I became Soames and you became Moxon . . . you didn't mind, did you, Watson?' He looked at me with genuine concern.

'Of course not, Holmes, but you surprise me by sensing there is a mystery connected with the old clockmaker's death. It all seemed to begin when we heard that raven, tick tocking.'

Holmes did not reply but continued puffing away, then asked, 'Watson, describe to me the symptoms of a heart attack.'

I deduced it was in connection with the clockmaker's death.

'Well, Holmes, sometimes there are no warnings and the victim is struck down and within seconds is dead. At other times, the victim has many small attacks over as many months, culminating with a massive attack which causes death.'

'Capital, Watson . . . they agree with my own layman's knowledge. Now describe to me the symptoms experienced by the victim of a massive heart attack, just prior to death.' I thought for a moment before replying.

'The victim sweats and then feels pain in the region of the chest. The pains become worse, it is as though a steel band is tightening around it. This can last for minutes or in some cases an hour or so. The pain becomes excruciating, unbearable . . . then it is all over.' Holmes made no remark, but just puffed at his pipe, the blue smoke keeping the evening midges at bay. I couldn't help wondering what the morrow would bring, what game was afoot, or would it all turn out to be a mare's nest?

There was something magical about lying down to sleep that summer night. The windows were wide open wafting in the smells of new mown hay, the sounds of the church bells striking the hour and the lowing of a cow in a distant field. All so different from London and Baker Street.

I heard Holmes bid goodnight to mine host, having had a further late-night walk around the village. His door closed and I soon fell asleep.

In the morning Holmes was up before me, but only just. Our breakfast seemed enormous compared with Mrs Hudson's, and it was only the country air and exercise that enabled me to clear my plate. Afterwards we packed our rucksacks, thanked our host and paid our dues. We smoked a pipe and waited for Jim to take us to Nether Froggatt to view the clockmaker's cottage, the sun already promising a good day.

The village was awake, the milkmaids had already milked the cows which even now were sidling down the street, returning to their pastures. A young boy with a dog brought up the rear. At the smithy, the blacksmith was pumping up and down his bellows to heat the first iron of the day and a horse was tied up and waiting to be shod. As the clock struck the hour of nine o'clock our faithful carrier and guide, Jim, brought the trap to a halt and bid us good morning. Holmes threw his rucksack into the trap and clambered aboard. I followed but not as spritely.

I noticed Holmes looked ahead, but without seeing. His mind, I knew, was on other things, I recognised the signs. When Jim and I conversed, Holmes remained silent. I knew he could not wait to arrive at the cottage and get to grips with the case of the clockmaker's death. It had been a pleasant drive, Jim setting us down on time outside the church. We gave him a generous tip and were genuinely sorry to bid him farewell. He turned the trap around, and waving goodbye was away at a good trot. We waited no more than a few minutes before the vicar could be seen walking through the churchyard towards us. 'A fine morning, gentlemen. I see you have your rucksacks packed, ready to continue your holiday after viewing the cottage.'

Holmes eased his straps. 'Yes, it is indeed a fine morning, vicar; the village is a hive of activity, I see.'

'Yes, they believe in the old adage of making hay whilst the sun shines. This way then, gentlemen.' We did not arouse much curiosity as we strolled with the vicar through the village. Attired in our rambling clothes and rucksacks we were just two more visitors, enjoying the views and fresh air, conversing with their vicar. The clockmaker's cottage was on the periphery of the village, off the main road and by the side of a wood.

It was a very small cottage, just two rooms and no upstairs. Stone built and roofed with pantiles which had at some time replaced the thatch, it sat squat and solid. A single chimney and one door; the basic requirements, but several small windows on three sides, and ivy grew up the walls onto the roof giving it a pleasant rustic attraction. A privy stood at the end of the garden under the trees.

As we reached the door, the sound of 'kwark, kwark' was heard in the upper branches of the closest tree. 'Kwark, kwark,' cried the raven, followed by 'tick tock, tick tock, tick tock' and again that harsh guttural foreign word 'Kiefernzapfen, kiefernzapfen, kiefernzapfen.'

Holmes slipped the rucksack off his back, placed it on the ground, opened it and took out a small parcel, the remains of his enormous breakfast we had been served. Sausage, liver, kidney and half a slice of bread. These he threw onto the ground under the tree. The raven who had been watching us with beady eyes, cocked its head on one side and flew down, walked with a sailor's gait and began eating the scraps. It appeared even larger on the ground and that huge beak looked most formidable.

The vicar watched the scene with us and then turned to unlock the door, saying, 'That bird has never once returned to the cottage. During all the time the doctor and I searched the cottage, we left the door ajar, but it never once came over the doorstep. Almost as though it knew its master was no longer here.' He swung the door back and we followed him in.

The room appeared even smaller than I had expected. Perhaps it was the low ceiling and the crowded-in furniture which made it seem so. On the whitewashed walls a few religious pictures hung, the text beneath in German. A small table was pushed up against the wall, a sideboard of pine wood and a huge Windsor chair by the fire side completed the furnishings. Oh, yes, the stand which the raven used to perch upon was beside the chair, also a padded small box used no doubt as a foot rest.

A door led into the other room partitioned off into a bedroom and kitchen-cum-workshop. The bedroom area was tiny, a single bed allowed just sufficient space to get in and out of it. A chest of drawers at the foot was the only other furniture.

However, it was the kitchen-cum-workshop that was a complete contrast. The workshop was a mass of shelves holding innumerable boxes of every size, wooden and cardboard. The contents of each box was written in German in thick black crayon on the outside. The lower shelves held open boxes of springs, cogs and screws of every description. A lathe and racks of tools stood on a workbench under a north-facing window to benefit from the light. Every inch of wall space was used. Several Black Forest cuckoo clocks were now mute and forlorn. From nails in the wall hung various clock faces, pendulums and still more hand tools.

We stood and stared for a while, taking in the scene. But before we began discussing the situation, the sound of a horse and trap could be heard. It halted outside and a few moments later through the doorway came a bewhiskered middle-aged man: top hat and gloves and of very smart appearance. The vicar greeted him.

'Good morning, Charles. Pleased to see you have not been delayed by some emergency or other.' The vicar turned to us. 'Let me introduce you, gentlemen. This is my friend and the local practitioner, Dr Charles Draycott, and this is Mr Soames and Mr Moxon.' We all shook hands and stood around for a few minutes discussing the poor clockmaker's demise, also the fact that no money of any great amount had been found. No bank account book, nothing.

The doctor placed his top hat carefully on a clear part of the work bench, saying, 'We spent the whole of one day systematically going through box after box, shelf after shelf; very unpleasant work indeed, but not a thing of real value did we discover, correct, vicar?'

The vicar agreed and added, 'We did find of course a few sovereigns in a box under the bench, and a few coins in his trouser pockets. But of the money he talked of, to build a row of almshouses and enough to keep them in repair in perpetuity, I am afraid there was none.'

There was silence whilst we all contemplated this.

I asked if he left a will.

The doctor answered. 'Yes, he did, just a simple sheet of paper affair, written by the schoolmaster and witnessed by him and a local farmer. The schoolmaster died some ten years ago, if my memory serves me right.' The vicar agreed.

I asked about the instructions in the will. Again the doctor replied. 'Oh! He appointed whoever was the vicar at the time of his death, to set up a trust to oversee the building of the almshouses, and sanction future repairs as necessary.'

The vicar added his voice. 'You see, this is why we wonder if he was robbed, bearing in mind the upset state of the living-room and of course the injury, although not serious, could have been caused when he tried to defend himself.'

I said, 'That is why you wondered if the gypsy had suspected the old man had money, and had come back some days later to rob him?'

The doctor took up the point. 'You see, he could have walked here from wherever they are encamped, done the deed, and made off, no one the wiser.'

We remained silent considering the theory. Meanwhile, during our conversation, Holmes had been prowling around, examining first the living-room, then the bedroom. Lastly of course, examining the black crayon writing indicating the contents in the boxes. One contained hundreds of cogs of all sizes. Another steel springs, an old shoe box was full of lengths of string for re-use: waste not want not.

He crouched down and examined a box full of clock weights he had pulled out from under the workbench. They were heavy weights, the type that hang on the chains of long-case clocks and cuckoo clocks. The weights were assorted shapes and sizes, dusty and dirty. He stood up and dusted his hands, pulled out a drawer and began examining the end, then reached inside the cavity, in case a note or something had been hidden.

Suddenly the vicar exclaimed aloud, 'I know of a place we have not looked . . . the chimney.' We followed him into the living-room. The grate was full of dead ashes. We stood around and watched as the vicar bent forward and peered upwards. Being very careful not to touch the encrusted soot of many years, he looked around, then withdrew his head. 'It's really difficult to examine it properly . . . it should be swept first. I think we should get old Ted to come and sweep it. We shall have to be present of course. If there's anything up there, Ted will find it.'

Just then I looked out of the window and caught sight at the end of the garden of the privy and garden shed. 'I suppose they have been searched?' They followed my gaze and the vicar replied slowly,

'No!' The doctor adding in a patronising tone, 'I can hardly imagine any sane person hiding anything of great value in a privy or garden shed.'

'Still we ought to look, I suppose,' persisted the vicar.

The three of us went up the path and examined the privy, which was of the two sitting side-by-side arrangement. The second seat contained a bucket of torn-up newspaper, ready for use. We removed both buckets and looked beneath, then replaced them. The garden hut was a small affair almost covered with ivy. A barrow, seed boxes, spade, fork, rake, a ball of twine, together with other small gardening paraphernalia completed the inventory. The doctor appeared more and more frustrated by the whole affair.

As we returned down the garden path, myself leading, he kept the vicar back and talked in whispers to him. I stood out of sight behind the door listening. I could not hear all that was said, only the odd word or two, here and there. But from the tone of the doctor's voice he appeared most agitated.

The doctor strode in, the vicar followed. His voice was loud and said with great authority, 'We should contact the police again and have this gypsy fellow tracked down.' The doctor glared at me as he spoke.

The vicar looked rather subdued. 'I suppose we should. After all, the old clockmaker must have had some money, or why would he have talked of almshouses, and made a will?'

The doctor, who was obviously the more dominant of the two, replied in a brisk tone, 'Of course we should. We should have done it the day after we searched the place. The police were lax. They won't be very pleased, but I will insist they find this gypsy fellow,' scornfully adding, 'that is if they can, the fellow will be miles away by now.'

The vicar looked crestfallen. Although the doctor had not said so in as many words, it was plain the vicar had been the one who had stayed the hand of the doctor at the time.

The voice of Holmes from the workshop called out, 'I wouldn't bother trying to track the gypsies down, they had nothing to do with it.'

The doctor looked even more annoyed and we followed him into the workshop to find Holmes leaning back against the clockmaker's workbench in a most casual manner. He said, 'We observed them in a clearing near Eyam village yesterday and spoke with them. I assure you they are completely innocent.'

The doctor I could see was quietly seething, but in a controlled voice asked, 'What reasons substantiate your view that they had nothing to do with it?'

Holmes smiled. 'If they had, doctor, they would hardly have stayed in the area, but would have put as many miles between themselves and the scene of the crime as possible. Would have walked the horse to exhaustion to achieve it.'

The doctor made no reply, no doubt inwardly agreeing with the very valid point Holmes had made. The vicar, I thought, looked relieved that the gypsy family had been exonerated.

Holmes continued, 'Shall I tell you what did happen here that night?'

He paused dramatically. 'You, doctor, diagnosed death was caused by heart failure, and you were quite correct.' I looked towards the doctor and his expression softened slightly. 'The clockmaker had eaten his supper, evident from the crumbs on his plate and dregs of cocoa in his cup. Sitting in his chair, with the raven by his side, he felt the beginning of the heart attack. Within minutes he was suffering the most excruciating pains in his chest. They grew worse, too painful to bear. It was then he realised death had come to take him. In his agony, still though able to reason, he remembered that in all his talks with you, vicar, he had never hinted at where the means to carry out his last wishes, his wealth, was to be found.' Holmes, who had been filling his pipe during this time and, striking a match on a nearby iron vice, continued:

'Like most of us, the clockmaker thought he would die in bed with time in plenty to make his arrangements. Sadly this was not so. He staggered to the door to open it, hoping the fresh air would help him. But the pain increased, now like an iron band around his chest. Leaving the door wide open, he lurched backwards again inside and reverting to his mother tongue, German, began shouting out aloud the same word over and over again . . . kiefernzapfen, kiefernzapfen, kiefernzapfen . . . screaming it in a last frantic effort to alert someone, anyone, who might understand what he was saying.

'He swayed and, with one hand held to his chest and the other supporting himself, went to the sideboard, picked up a pencil intending to scrawl a message on any piece of paper that came to hand, but the pencil point, under his claw-like grip, broke. He was desperate now. The last of his energy used up in ransacking the drawers you found open, in his desperate search for anything to write with, the stub of a pencil, a crayon or anything. He found nothing. Hardly now able to move, he lurched towards his chair still screaming, over and over again, the same German word, kiefernzapfen, kiefernzapfen, kiefernzapfen.

'The raven by now was frantic with

fear. Its beloved master's behaviour was beyond its understanding. The old man reached his chair and, in doing so, pulled over the raven's perch hitting his head on the sharp metal. In terror the horrified bird flew round and round the room as his master screamed out those strange words in a voice full of pain and suffering. Those were the last words the raven heard from its beloved master, before flying terrified through the open door into the night. The Grim Reaper had called and left. All was quiet now, the candle continued to flicker, keeping up its all-night vigil. Sometime during the night it went out. Like the old clockmaker, it had run its time.'

We were all silent. The picture painted by Holmes had captured the imagination of us all then; as though it had been listening, the raven screamed out those words of its dying master several times, then all was silent again.

'You see,' said Holmes, 'it still remembers those words screamed in those last terrifying moments, associating them with that awful night.' Holmes reached up and took down from a hook in the ceiling, the remains of a side of bacon, smoked no doubt over the fire in the other room. He strode out and threw it onto the grass by the back door. The raven glided down and began tearing at it with its powerful beak. Holmes returned to us in the workshop. The doctor and the vicar said nothing, I think they were overcome not only with what Holmes had described, but the way Holmes had spoken, so sure of his facts, one never questioned them, as though he had been an unseen observer.

Looking up at the low-beamed ceiling, Holmes puffed away at his pipe, then around at his audience and continued. 'My colleague and I came across a secondhand bookshop in Tideswell and I took the opportunity to look up in a German dictionary the word the raven had called out so many times. I guessed it was Teutonic and that the clockmaker in his distress and pain had reverted back to his mother tongue. What that word had meant I had no idea, but I felt that it must be important, if a dying man used his last breath to utter it.'

He paused and looked at us in turn. 'However, I was puzzled. The translation I finally arrived at after much research was 'The Pine Cones'.'

We each in turn repeated the words as though, by doing so, we might solve the puzzle of why a dying man would utter such words. We repeated the words over and over again to ourselves and each other, before looking again towards Holmes, still leaning against the bench, his pipe clenched in his mouth, the picture of a man in complete control of the situation.

'Yes, I too was as puzzled as you, until I happened to rummage about in this box of old clock weights. They are dusty, dirty and the paint is chipped on some. You see they are in all shapes and sizes.' He pointed to them, 'But it was on sorting through them I noticed that some of the weights were cast in the shape of fire tree cones, like the ones on the end of the chains hanging from the cuckoo clocks. The box contained ten such cones to be exact.' Holmes moved aside to reveal, laid out on the bench, the ten cones arranged like an angler might display his fish, in a row.

Each one shaped like a fir cone.

He removed his pipe and placed it on the bench. 'I found a strange thing about these weights . . . watch the weight of each one as I place it on this set of scales.'

Holmes placed them one at a time on the scales, all of us peering intently as he did so. The first six cones were approximately the same weight, twelve ounces. The seventh cone caused the scale to bump down heavily, so did the remaining three.

Holmes turned to us. 'Why, when they are all identical in shape and size, should four be heavier than the other six?'

We were silent, then the vicar said, 'They must be made from different metal.'

But the doctor brusquely remarked, 'It is obvious the six are of cast-iron and the other four of lead.'

Smiling, I thought deliberately, Holmes replied, 'Almost right, but not quite.

219

What metal is heavier than lead, in fact almost twice as heavy?'

We were again silent, one could almost hear the concentration, whilst Holmes waited patiently like a schoolmaster for the correct answer.

I said, 'You don't mean . . . ' I paused almost afraid to say it and raise false hopes, especially in the vicar. Holmes encouraged me, 'Go on.'

I gasped out, 'They are gold . . . they are gold, aren't they?'

Holmes replied, 'Top marks . . . under the grime and dust, they are solid gold. I have run a file down them and removed some of the paint; you can see the gold revealed.'

We each in turn handled the heavy cone weights and observed the glint of bright gold. Each one made of solid gold, and worth a fortune. We seemed speechless at the turn of events. Holmes had sprung it upon us suddenly, like a magician pulling a rabbit from a hat.

'What better way to hide away his wealth than disguised as old dusty clock weights in an open wooden box which once contained soap? We must remember, as the vicar mentioned only the other day, he was German and over many hundreds of years invading armies have fought back and forth across Europe. It has been the practice for people to hide away their valuables, jewellery, silver plate and gold, by burying it under the ground. Later, when the looting armies had passed and the war was over, they would unearth it again.'

He pointed to the cones, 'The old clockmaker cast these weights from the mould he made from the lead cones and cast these four of solid gold. Afterwards, he painted them and allowed dust and dirt to gather, so as to appear and look just like the others in the box. He didn't need to bury them in the ground; what thief would carry away a heavy box of clock weights of minimum value when he could so easily lift off the wall a valuable cuckoo clock?

'My colleague will confirm that one of my many interests over the years has been gold. The history of gold and the crimes and murder committed to possess

221

this international currency. Gold has a specific gravity of 19.3 and is nearly twice as heavy as lead which has a specific gravity of only 11.34. Lode gold is mined whereas alluvial is panned from streams and rivers and it is all initially cast into ingots or bars. It can be cast in any shape or form, hence our gold cones.

'Gold never tarnishes it is malleable making it an ideal dental filling, for those that can afford it, of course. Gentlemen, I could talk for hours about gold, but, suffice to say, your humble, kind benefactor has left you more, much more, than your trust will need to build its almshouses and keep them maintained.'

All of us were so overcome by events that we were seemingly, at first, left speechless and listening to Holmes trotting out his facts in such a matter-of-fact way had completely mesmerised us. But after getting over the welcome shock and having a little time to digest the situation, we all began congratulating him on his brilliant detective work. The vicar left the room and returned a moment later holding up a pencil and an envelope. 'Look, it's as you described the events of that night, here is an envelope and the pencil with a broken point.' They looked towards Holmes with awe and admiration.

The doctor's attitude towards Holmes was now not only civil but contrite, asking him, as a means of conveying his change of opinion, if he thought the clockmaker's injury had been caused when he struck his head on the raven's perch?

'Yes,' replied Holmes. 'If some time before then, we would have expected to find blood all over the room. On striking and upsetting the perch he gashed his head and it bled all over his neck, collar and shoulder until, a few minutes later, his heart stopped and so, of course, the bleeding.'

It was decided that the doctor and the vicar would take the gold straight away to the bank in Bakewell for safe keeping. The cottage was locked up again and we all stood around saying our goodbyes. The vicar, especially, was overjoyed and confessed that without Soames's help, the mystery would never have been solved and the village deprived of the old people's almshouses. 'The village can never thank you enough and I am sure the clockmaker is looking down upon us at this very moment, satisfied that his wishes will be carried out.'

Holmes thanked them in return and, addressing the vicar, remarked, 'I hope in your sermon next Sunday, vicar, you will mention who is the real person to thank, the fellow in the shining black coat up there in the tree. He provided the real clue. I feel everyone in the village will see he gets the very best of the table scraps as his reward.'

The doctor took up the reins and with the vicar beside him reached over and shook our hands, saying, 'Thank you once again, gentlemen, it has been an honour and a pleasure to have met you both. You have proved the truth in the old saying 'Every man to his job'. I sincerely apologise for doubting your abilities. Left to me, I would have had the police searching for the gypsy family and we would never have discovered the gold.'

'You are quite right, doctor, every man to his trade; this is how civilisation has reached the zenith it has today. Every trade and profession improves upon the last. It was just fortunate my colleague and I were around to help, that's all. Our reward is knowing that many old residents of the village will end their lives together here in the almshouses, instead of in some unknown town workhouse, with husband and wife separated and miserable.'

The doctor looked pleased and replied, 'Perhaps we could call the almshouses after you gentlemen, as a means of remembering your services?'

Holmes raised his hand. 'No, no. But perhaps they could be named 'Ravensdale Almshouses' in memory of the little fellow in the black coat.'

# Sherlock Holmes and the Trophy Room

My friend, Sherlock Holmes, was in a good mood. Mrs Hudson, our landlady, had cooked us her usual excellent breakfast, the papers had been read and the sun was already up and shining through the windows. The promise of another perfect day.

'You know, Watson, I feel it in my bones that this glorious morning will bring us forth an interesting case.'

I looked across at Holmes and nodded. 'Shall we delay our walk through the park a while then, say half an hour, in case this interesting case should come to our door?'

Holmes went to the window and looked down into Baker Street, busy already with people coming and going. He stroked his long chin and his eyes reminded me as always of a hawk, bright and missing nothing. A few moments later he turned to me.

'If I'm not mistaken, Watson, from the coat of arms I observe on the coach door stopping outside our humble abode, our problem comes hotfoot in the form of a peer of the realm.'

There were voices outside the door. One was of Mrs Hudson, the other deep and booming. A moment later a knock at the door and Holmes went to answer it. Mrs Hudson stood there, and then stepped backwards, to allow the stranger to come forward.

'A gentleman to see you, Mr Holmes.'

The stranger was a huge mountain of a man, in his middle thirties, with a military bearing. His chest massive, his face rugged. He thrust out his hand and said, 'Viscount Siddems . . . I have the pleasure, I believe, of addressing Mr Sherlock Holmes and,' he looked across the room to where I was standing, still holding a morning paper, 'Dr Watson.'

Holmes, although this was hardly necessary, our visitor being far from the timid sort, ushered him in and, as was usual, put his visitor at ease. The viscount was clearly not a troubled man. He smiled and appeared happy and relaxed. Holmes said, 'Well, sir, it is obvious that the problem you have is not a serious one. Perhaps intriguing more than sinister.' The face of our visitor creased into a further smile.

'Then you have heard all about the thefts from my trophy room?'

'No,' said Holmes, 'but you appear in such good humour that it could not be sinister, or you would not smile so freely. Believe me, many who consult my good friend and I come with worried faces, and often are on the point of despair.'

The visitor smiled again. 'No, indeed. My problem is not one of despair or serious really. Perplexing, intriguing, yes.'

Holmes settled back into his chair. 'That is good to hear. On a fine morning like this, we should be involved in a puzzle to excite our minds, not depressed, with the worried face of a client at his wits' end. Please speak freely. I shall interrupt you only if necessary to clear up any point I need to clarify.'

Against the background sounds of the street vendors, a rather raucous oyster seller and the clip-clop noise of a dozen horses, the noble viscount unfolded his story.

'I was with my regiment many years in India, and whilst out there I became a fair player of polo. I not only collected a large number of shields, but won some of the finest trophies a man could wish to complete for. I might say, I was proud to come back to the old country with such a collection.

'My father died soon after my return, and it was then I decided to build a trophy room-cum-armour museum, to display the Japanese and oriental body armour I had collected over the years out there.

'It was the type of place, you know, where a man can retire to with his cronies, away from the womenfolk, if you gather what I mean. It was whilst I was wondering about where to build the trophy house that I was burgled.

'A couple of trophies were taken, but the police soon arrested the scoundrel and the property was recovered. However, it did make me think, if my collection attracted thieves, then I should make it thief-proof.

'The top and bottom of the matter was, I had the trophy house built a few hundred yards away from the Hall, and surrounded it with man-traps, trip-wires to set off shot guns, and a flock of geese. I don't do things by halves.'

I looked a little surprised at the mention of a flock of geese. Holmes saw the look of surprise on my face and leaning forward, remarked, 'The geese are to warn of undesirable intruders. The Romans, two thousand years ago, used them as watchdogs. The slightest unusual sound will set them off honking.' I was aware of this, but surprised all the same.

I nodded my head to signify I understood and the viscount continued.

'I spent a fortune in time and money both on the trophy room and on making it secure from burglars. You see, during daylight hours it was safe; any intruder would have been seen, but at night without the trip-wires, man-traps and geese, I couldn't be sure.

'However, I was confident everything was done to make it safe and secure. As I say, it cost a lot of time and money. In fact the farmers who rent their land from me grumbled to my agent, saying I was neglecting things because of it. Be that as it may, I wasn't having anyone burgle my precious trophies.

'Well, you can imagine the shock when, one day, I visited the trophy room and found the door unlocked, and one of my prize trophies missing.

'I had my gamekeepers and gardeners test every trip-wire and shotgun. Then there were the geese; how had the intruder got past the geese? I can tell you, Mr Holmes, I was very annoyed; it was a complete mystery how the burglar had managed it.

'A few weeks passed and then it happened again. I couldn't believe it. I increased the trophy room security; put more man-traps down, more guns, added bells to the trip-wires to tinkle and make it more difficult. Why, on a windy night the gamekeepers would be constantly alerted; the bells you see, the wind would make them tinkle most of the time.

'Well, just as I considered that I had beaten them, it happened again. Another prize trophy was taken. I can tell you, Mr Holmes, I was furious, yet at the same time, I couldn't help but admire the sheer brilliance of the thief. He has me beaten, yes, beaten.'

He looked at Holmes and leaned back in his chair to await comment. Holmes took the pencil he had been playing with and placed it on the desk by his chair.

'A most intriguing case.' Then, standing up, as though indicating he had already wasted valuable time just listening to the account, said, 'I think the only way we shall solve this crime is to visit the scene. When can we come?'

The viscount was surprised at Holmes's immediate action. I was not. Knowing my friend of old, I sensed that once he had the bit between his teeth, so to speak, he would not be content until the mystery was solved.

We travelled down by the fast evening train and listened with interest to the tales told by the viscount of his years in India. I was able to relate to them, comparing them with the time I also had spent there.

The viscount excused himself for a minute and disappeared into the corridor, so I took the opportunity to ask Holmes the exact order of ranking of a viscount. You see, although Holmes always considered me the expert on ranking concerning the army and navy, I was always adrift somewhat when it came to the nobility.

Holmes cocked an ear towards the corridor and said, 'A viscount, my dear Watson, is a member of the fourth order of the British peerage, ranking between an earl and a baron, the title dating back to the reign of Henry VI.'

'Thank you, Holmes, only I do like to know where he stands in the order of merit.'

'Quite so, quite so. Ha! Here he returns now.'

So engrossed were we that I think we

were all surprised when the train stopped and the porter was shouting out the name of the station. We clambered out, a little stiff from sitting, and walked along the platform towards the exit. The train disappeared in a swirl of steam and smoke, the little red light on the guard's van soon lost as it gathered speed.

His Lordship's coach was waiting outside the station entrance, and soon we were making our way along country roads, the lamps of the coach lighting up the hedges as we passed.

Twenty minutes later we turned in between two large ornate iron gates, and the sound of gravel could be heard under the wheels.

We spent a pleasant evening after dinner in the company of the viscount and his lady, but all too soon it was bedtime and we made our way to our allotted rooms.

The next morning proved bright and sunny. Holmes ate his breakfast quickly and I could tell he was eager to visit the scene of the crime, the trophy room.

This we soon did, the viscount leading

the way, accompanied at a respectful distance by the head gamekeeper and two of his men.

Here I must describe for the reader the trophy house. It had been designed by one of the best architects of the day, built of stone and its design was classical, borrowing heavily upon Grecian and Roman-style features.

The only windows to let light in were those on the elevation facing the Hall, thus allowing more wall space inside upon which body armour and trophies could be displayed.

It was a handsome edifice and, it had to be admitted, gave added interest to the vista in the same way many a folly had been erected to add interest to a landscape.

Holmes examined the ground thoroughly, the head keeper and his men unloading the shotguns to enable the triggers to be tested. Having examined the fortifications outside, Holmes stopped at the door to the trophy house.

'May I examine the key, my Lord? Ah! Chubb, 57 St Paul's Churchyard,

London,' he read stamped on the key. 'A good firm, but unfortunately even the best keys can be copied. I see, too, you installed only one lock . . . any reason why?'

'Yes, you see I reasoned that as no one could get as far as the door, there was little sense in fixing more than one lock; more to unfasten and fasten when visiting the house.'

Holmes nodded and said, 'And each time a trophy had been removed, the door was found to be closed, but unlocked?'

'Yes, that is correct.'

We entered the trophy house and on each wall was hung the trophies won, and the body armour collected, in far-off countries by the viscount. Shields and silver cups were to be seen everywhere. Holmes prowled around looking with his keen eyes, then he turned to the viscount.

'I find it very strange that the Hall which contains many really valuable things in the way of paintings and silver, which I took the opportunity last evening of examining, is very poorly secured. Why, it would take only a very amateur burglar no trouble at all to break in and carry off far more valuable things than your trophies.'

He continued after reading the inscription engraved on a particularly fine shield.

'I suspect there is a reason for taking your trophies. After all, if the thief spent such great effort in overcoming your defences, he would surely have taken more than just one trophy. Why did he not pocket those small cups there, for instance,' pointing to a shelf, 'and make his visit more worthwhile.'

He paced up and down deep in thought.

'No, I don't believe we are looking for someone local. It could be a friend who wishes to pit his skill against your own, just for the sheer fun of it.'

The good viscount looked hard at Holmes, but did not reply.

We left the trophy house and very carefully made our way back to the perimeter where the geese were. I was not keen on stepping over the trip-wires, the slightest mistake would have discharged one of those guns, with terrible consequences.

Holmes turned to the noble lord and suggested that we now continue the investigation on our own, and that we would all meet again over lunch. And so it was agreed and the viscount strode away to examine some new man-trap that had been delivered that morning.

Holmes shook his head slowly from side to side.

'I am afraid that whatever traps he puts down, our intruder will overcome them.'

We walked about a hundred yards and suddenly Holmes stopped and turned about.

'See, Watson, the trophy house is sited hundreds of yards from the nearest tree. Right out in the open parkland. That cuts across any theory that the intruder may have used a rope to swing across the circle of defences.

'Then there are the geese; penned at night in the outer circle of the enclosure. They would set up an unholy honking and alert the gamekeepers who, we are told, during the night hours are always nearby.' He glanced over my shoulder. 'Ah! If I am not mistaken that figure approaching us is Mr Wilson, the estate manager. I have some questions for him.'

Mr Wilson was a tall thin man with a thinning thatch of grey hair. He had been with the viscount's father since he began as a garden boy. He looked after the estate, hiring and sometimes firing, men as he saw fit. He was considered hard, but fair; stood no nonsense. You either did your job to his satisfaction or you were dismissed.

Holmes smiled and bid the estate manager good morning.

'You no doubt have a few questions, Mr Holmes . . . I shall try to answer them as honestly as I am able.'

Holmes laughed. 'I am sure you will . . . it is about the workers on the estate that I wish to question you.'

Mr Wilson nodded and stroked his jaw. 'I see. Well, go ahead.'

'Firstly, who are the ones you have set to work most recently?'

He did not reply immediately, giving

the question some thought. 'Well, the young Jackson lad we took on the gardening staff last month was the most recent. His father, Bill, also works as a gardener, has done since he left school.'

Holmes smiled and said, 'And other members of staff recently appointed?'

The estate manager viewed some distant deer nibbling grass. They were the viscount's pride and joy but, I suspected, not his from the look that passed momentarily across his face. 'Well, there is Johnson who does a lot of the odd jobs and helps out in the kitchen. He worked for one of the local farmers, but reduced his workforce; he was lucky to find a job here.'

Holmes cut in quickly. 'What about persons employed recently who have no local connections?'

Mr Wilson nodded towards the Hall. 'Ah! Well, there's Stevens, the butler. Came with good recommendations from his last position. His Lordship interviewed him, of course. Been with us almost three years, I should say.'

'About as long as his Lordship has

been home from India then?' remarked Holmes.

'Yes, I should say so. The previous butler retired after the death of his Lordship's father.'

Holmes turned towards the trophy house. 'I suppose the construction and security, guns, trip-wires, geese and the like have put extra work on you and your staff?' Holmes watched his face and saw a look of weariness flicker just for a moment across it; then it was replaced by an alertness, as though realising he had revealed his most private feelings, was now determined that the rest of the conversation would give nothing away. Holmes continued.

'Do I gather that you think his Lordship has spent too much time and money on his . . . pet hobby, and not enough time on more important things, like the managing of the estate?'

Mr Wilson drew himself up and gave Holmes an unfriendly look. 'I did not say so. What his Lordship does is entirely his own affair. I merely carry out his instructions.'

It was obvious Holmes had touched a sore point and had annoyed him.

'If there are no more questions, Mr Holmes, I will be gone. I have matters to attend to.'

'Just one more question,' said Holmes. 'The names of the workers who helped his Lordship lay out the traps, wires and guns.'

Wilson produced a list from his pocket. 'I thought you might want to know that, so I made a note of them for you. There are eight all told. The first on the list is Brown; been with the family as a gardener since leaving school.

'The next is old blind Jim Roberts. An old army man. Rather tragic how he lost his sight; was captured on the Indian northwest frontier by tribesmen. They staked him out in the hot sun for three days. When they found him, he was in a bad way, they say; but he recovered, all except his sight. His Lordship's father gave him his present job when he was invalided out of the army.

'Then there is the third on the list. Parsons, a gamekeeper, obviously handy with things like shotguns, traps and trip-wires. He's a very practical man. His Lordship took him off his normal duties to help. Then there is Smith, a coachman, again handy with his hands, so his Lordship took him too.'

We listened patiently whilst the other four names were listed. All were old and trusted workers.

Holmes bade the estate manager good morning and we continued our walk.

'Well, we appear to have ruffled the feathers of our good Mr Wilson. Obviously he considered the use of so many of his men taken off their duties to set traps, trip-wires and guns as so much waste of time and money, but was too loyal to admit it.'

'And the others?' I said.

'All good solid respectable workers, I imagine; most of them, as you heard, had been with the family for years. I rather fancy some unknown person we have yet to hear of, one of his Lordship's cronies, a fellow officer from his Indian days, may be at the bottom of it.' He stepped around a muddy part of the pathway. 'You know, someone who was willing to risk life and limb to pit his wits against his Lordship.' I agreed it was a possibility.

'I think I shall have a word with the butler, see if he can supply a few names for us to investigate. It might be a short-cut to solving the case, rather than trying to work out how the thief overcame the formidable barrier of security.'

We watched the geese feeding on the grass outside their night quarters for a while, then Holmes went in search of the butler, whilst I walked down to the lake to try a spot of fishing with a rod and line lent me by his Lordship.

I caught a couple of good perch and then returned to the Hall for lunch. Over the meal, Holmes remarked that he understood that, this Saturday, the village show was to be held.

His Lordship swallowed the food in his mouth, and replied.

'Yes, it's a great event. The workers on the estate and everyone in the village look forward to it. There are prizes for best jams, best vegetables, best rabbits, you know the sort of thing; and, of course, events.'

Holmes said, 'And feats of skill and daring, I hear.'

His Lordship poised his fork midway. 'If you refer to the prize I give to the village lad who can get furthest into my trophy house fortifications, then you're right.'

I gasped and before really thinking, said, 'But surely that is highly dangerous, sir. I mean, one of those boys could set off a trap or a shotgun.'

His Lordship laughed. 'No, no, Dr Watson. The traps are all sprung so they cannot hurt anyone, and the guns are disarmed; no shot in them. The boys are blindfolded and they have to try and get as near the trophy house as possible, without tripping over a wire or tinkling a bell.'

Holmes asked, 'And have any managed to get all the way to the trophy house wall yet?'

'Bless you, no. The best was a lad who got halfway, so it is proof of the effectiveness of my defences.'

'Not quite . . . otherwise we would not be here,' replied Holmes.

'Quite right, Mr Holmes, quite right.' The viscount looked a little abashed.

Holmes continued, 'And after the show, all the man-traps are reset and the guns loaded again?' His Lordship agreed.

'Yes, and don't forget the geese. At night, young Sanders, the stable lad, herds them all into the inner compound to sleep. No one can get by them without waking them up . . . ' He looked rather foolishly at Holmes, realising the fallacy of his boast, yet again.

When we were by ourselves after dinner, enjoying the use of his Lordship's library, I asked Holmes if he had gathered any useful information from the butler.

'Much, much, Watson. But it will take time to follow it up; for that we shall need to return to London, for it is there most of his Lordship's friends reside, but not all. One or two live close by, very close by indeed. They visit him, I understand, mostly at weekends. They swap stories and anecdotes about their old life out in India. I should imagine about the polo matches and sports events they took part in, that sort of thing. Young army officers the world over get up to some pranks, as you no doubt did yourself, Watson.' I had to agree, thinking about some I had taken part in.

'So you think it likely that it could be one of them behind it all?' Holmes did not reply, but got up from his chair and went over to the window, which had a view of the trophy house in the distance. The geese were now penned-up in the outer perimeter, the inner containing all the traps, wires and guns, of course.

Holmes turned around, sat down, filled his pipe and puffed away, blue smoke drifting in clouds about him. At last he spoke.

'Your know, Watson, the thing that worries me most about this case is the geese. They are creatures of a most sensitive nature. The slightest unfamiliar sound, as you are aware, will set them off honking in a most unholy manner.'

'Could they have been drugged?' I

ventured to suggest. 'The old poacher's trick, you know, of putting down raisins soaked in brandy to catch pheasants. The pheasants eat up the raisins, go up into the tree to roost and later drop down to the ground, drunk with the brandy, ready for the poachers to quietly gather up during the night.'

'No, Watson, I'm afraid not. I thought of that, but the young lad Sanders, who has the job of both penning and releasing them at sunrise each morning into the park, informed me that on no occasion have the geese appeared doped or drunk. They have all been alert and ready to be let out. If an attempt at doping them had taken place, some of the geese would have been bound to have eaten more of the doped raisins than others, appearing still drowsy the following morning.'

Holmes settled down for a catnap, while I looked along the library shelves for something to read.

'You don't think it is Wilson, the estate manager, do you Holmes?'

I was rather surprised myself at my sudden speaking out aloud my thoughts.

He opened his eyes and looked at me for a few moments before replying.

'I, too, have considered him as a possible candidate. Consider this, Watson. He is in a very difficult position, trying to please his employer, and yet at the same time, being the whipping boy for everything that goes wrong and needs attention on the estate. He sees what requires to be done, but is denied the authority to do anything about it, so busy is he with carrying out the whims and wishes of his Lordship. Did you notice how he stared at the deer grazing the grass when we spoke to him?'

'Yes, I thought he viewed them with irritation almost. I didn't feel he was too happy about them.'

'You are right. I learned from the man who is in charge of the estate sawmill, that the introduction of deer onto the estate is another of his Lordship's innovations. The sawyer has had to provide from the estate timber miles of fencing to keep the deer contained to that part of the estate, from where best they can be viewed from the Hall.'

'But why does his Lordship wish to see deer grazing?' I was perplexed.

'I understand it is the latest fad of some of the landed gentry, the ladies mostly, to give a sylvan look to the vista, as they and their guests gather for afternoon tea in their fine country houses.'

'So, in an act of frustration, Wilson decides to vent his rage on . . . '

'No, Watson, I don't think so. He is the kind of man who, although thwarted and baulked in carrying out his duties, would never, I repeat, never, carry out such an action of revenge. It is not in the nature of the man.

'I found it most interesting talking to the sawyer. He informed me that the invention of the circular saw came about when a workman in Mansfield, Nottinghamshire, you know the shire county of the legendary Robin Hood, cut the teeth on the edge of a circular piece of cardboard, spun it on axle and cut a carrot in two with it. From a small simple idea grew the huge steel circular saws like the one on this estate, and now used all over the world.'

Holmes sank back into his chair again and catnapped on, whilst I found a book on pike fishing which filled the time before hearing the dinner gong being struck.

That evening, having dined well with the noble lord and his lady, we walked down to the village inn to partake of the good ale and, knowing Holmes's habits, to mix with the locals in the hope of picking up any information.

The inn was packed, which rather surprised me. The head gardener came across to speak with us, and then the head gamekeeper came to ask us to have a drink. The locals were good mannered and did not stare directly at the famous Sherlock Holmes, but contented themselves from time to time, with sidelong glances. Holmes remarked, 'The inn is very full. Is it like this most evenings?'

The head gamekeeper lowered his drinking mug. 'Oh, no bless you!' 'Tis the show on Saturday that brings them in. They're here to find out who stands a chance of winning, what the other chap is likely to exhibit and such like.'

The head gardener agreed. 'Tis a rare old show, Mr Holmes. Be you stopping to see it?'

Holmes looked from one to the other. 'A lot depends upon my being able to bring the case to a successful conclusion.'

'Be you any nearer, Mr Holmes, like clearing it up?' asked the gamekeeper.

Holmes replied that he was still investigating and had not yet finished interviewing everyone.

Many of the locals in the inn we recognised, having spoken with them when walking around the estate. There was Shaw, one of the grooms, talking to old blind Jim Roberts. In front of them Jim had a huge parsnip which the groom was turning over and weighing in his hand. 'When t'other gardeners knock off from their gardening when it gets dusk, old Jim just carries on; 'tis all the same to 'im,' said the head gardener.

'They brings in samples to show each other, it's a bit of a bluff really. They sometimes brings in a poor specimen to show the other chap, and the other chap thinks, if that's the best he can show, he needn't bother too much when he gets his own stuff ready for the show. Only to be beaten like, because the other chap brings his really good stuff in on the day of the show. At other times a chap will bring his very best stuff, hoping to dishearten the other chap from not showing. It's a bit of lark really; each knows what the other's up to, but it's all part of the fun.'

As we talked, we were pleasantly aware that a mouth-organ was being played and the sound of rapid hand-clapping to accompany it was coming from an ever-widening circle of patrons at the far end of the room.

In the centre of the circle a most agile and energetic dancer was performing what can only be described as a cossack dance, popular now on the stage of some of the music-halls. He danced with vigour and vitality; his shirt partly pulled out from his trousers gave it a Russian blouse look.

His audience clapped louder and louder, faster and faster, until the finale, when he walked on his hands, back-flipped and pirouetted into the air.

There was prolonged applause as the dancer, a rather handsome dark-haired man in his middle forties, accepted a drink from the landlord. I turned to the head gardener and remarked, 'By Jove, that was a fine display of dancing. Is he a local man?'

'Oh, yes, sir!' he pointed with the stem of his pipe and exclaimed, 'that's our Jack Page. He's a real Jack the lad if ever there wus one . . . born here in the village . . . ain't that right, Harry?' turning to the head gamekeeper who readily agreed.

'Yes, he's the very best of men is Jack . . . left the village when he was a young man. A real jack-of-all-trades is Jack . . . has been a jockey, seaman, pawnbroker's clerk . . . trod the boards for a few years all over the country . . . and lastly, afore he came back to the village, performed in a circus.'

Holmes laughed softly and remarked, 'I imagine, too, from what I see here, he's a very popular man?'

'Aye, he's popular all reet, and up at

the Hall too.' Holmes asked in what way. The head gardener turned and said, 'You tell it, Harry; you was there at the time.' Harry put down his pint pot.

'Well, it wus the first year he had returned to the village, and he was helping at the summer fair . . . set up a coconut stall . . . only he used turnips instead. Now understand this, our Jack is a born talker . . . wit comes out of his mouth natural like. Anyway, her Ladyship happens to stop at his stall, an' they get talking. Jack talks to her like she wus just a village lass, and she laughs and talks, and talks and laughs, fair taken with him she was.' He took a long swig of ale, wiped his moustache with the back of his hand before continuing.

'I wus at the next stall, earwiggin,' and Jack drops out that he wore once in the circus. 'Oh! aye,' sez 'ee, 'it was great walking through the streets . . . it was a free show for towns-folk, see. They cheered and waved . . . wagons of lions, tigers and elephants and hosses walking with the dwarfs, clowns, and me on me tall stilts wearing striped trousers and top hat.'

' 'Oh!' sez her Ladyship, 'so you walked on stilts, did you?'

'Jack replied, 'Aye, but I had to pack that in, it wore my legs, you see.'

' 'Oh, dear!' sez her Ladyship, 'What was wrong?'

' 'Well, I went to see local doctor in the town we were performing in like, an'he examined me legs an' he sez, 'I'm afraid it's bad news.' I sez, 'Tell me the worst, Doctor.' '

' 'Well,' he sez, 'I'm afraid you've got woodworm in both legs.' '

'Well, I thought her Ladyship 'ud never stop laughing, tears flowed down her cheeks and somewun fetched a chair for her to sit on. Well, after that he was a regular visitor up at the Hall.

'Whenever her Ladyship had a party of guests, she allus asked Jack to come, as a guest mind. He made 'em all laugh, did Jack, him being so jovial, witty and full of glee, but she allus made it well worth his while, besides all the good food and drink he had.

256

'Aye! She thinks the world of him, so do everywun in the village . . . allus willing to lend a hand . . . and he's a very clever chap too . . . can fix most things . . . thinks quick like.' It was a wonderful anecdote and both Holmes and I enjoyed listening to it.

The head gardener nodded towards the end of the room where Jack was sitting.

'It wus his quick thinking that saved a little lass a few years back who had fallen through the ice in the big lake one winter. When everywun else wus panicking and wondering what to do to get her out, Jack had decided quick like and fetched a couple of shepherd's sheep hurdles, an' laying flat on one, he shoved other wun in front of him, then he crawled on that wun, and pulled other wun round to his front, an' kept on doing this till he reached her.' He paused to sip from his pot.

Holmes took out his pipe and remarked, 'A most admirable enterprising fellow indeed, what say you, Watson?' I readily agreed.

'And that's not all either. When he

brought her back to the bank, she wore lifeless and like a block of ice. Most said she wore dead and were in dismay, but not Jack. He wrapped his jacket around her and ran all the way to her home. Tells her mother and grandmother to take her upstairs, take their clothes off and get into bed naked with the little 'un between 'em.

'Then he gets neighbours to fetch their own bedding and pile it on top of 'em. That way their body heat thawed her out slowly like. After a while she began to move and they could feel her breathing, God bless her. They all lay together while she slept. Three days later that little lass wus playin' with her brother and sisters, as right as rain. Folks round here reckon it wore nowt short of a miracle. Aye, it wore a gladsome day when Jack returned to village.'

We agreed, and looked more closely with added interest at Jack the lad as he and his cronies put aside their pots to clear the table for a game of dominoes. The general laughter and bonhomie of the inn was good to see amongst these ruddy brown-faced countrymen.

Holmes and I found two stools to sit on. 'A most admirable account, my dear Watson, I fancy we . . . '

He was interrupted when a rather thick-set hunk of a man entered the room. He was the prize fighter who would be offering five pounds to any man to knock him down at the show. A little man standing near me whispered behind his hand, 'They say he soaks 'is 'ands in vinegar to make 'em 'ard as iron.'

We stayed a while longer, having a word here and there and generally enjoying the company. However, time was getting on and we had decided to enjoy a walk across the park before turning in for the night. During the walk, I asked if Holmes had formed any ideas about the case.

'Not yet, Watson. I find the case most baffling, not just in one aspect, but several. I feel that until we get back to London and have a chance to learn more about his Lordship's friends, we shall not solve the mystery . . . however . . . now there are other avenues to explore.' He did not enlarge on this.

The moon had risen and we were enjoying the walk back when suddenly, out of the night sky, swept a white form. It seemed to drift and float, then drop down; a moment later it rose from the ground and flapped away. We stood still, not speaking, until the barn owl was lost to sight in the trees. It had been a most breathtaking display of how the silent killer of the night finds its prey, but just another mouse supper for the barn owl.

We reached the ornamental garden situated behind the Hall and, because the night was warm and the moon so brilliant, we decided to take the opportunity to sit awhile in the beautiful surroundings. Stoking up our pipes, we enjoyed the quiet and magic of the garden. Far away in the woods a nightingale sang its heart out, whilst bats flittered above our heads. I took my pipe out and rested it on the arm of the bench seat.

'In the list of suspects, Holmes, have you now added Jack the lad, thinking about how he might have used his stilts some way?' Holmes was silent for a while.

'Yes, I have, Watson, considering it may have been a scheme hatched between her Ladyship and him.'

'Really, with what motive pray?'

'Oh! She might have become tired of his Lordship's obsession with his hobby. Trophies, oriental armour, guns, trip-wires and man-traps are hardly likely to interest her or her friends. She was perhaps hoping the thefts may have been the means to discourage his further interest ... we never know do we, old chap, the real relationship between people? Married people, especially the upper classes, often present a false picture of harmony to their friends and neighbours than actually exists in private.'

'True, Holmes, true. Arranged marriages of royalty through the ages were made to obtain power and good alliances with other states, whilst the nobility arrange them with a view to keeping their estates and perhaps enlarging them.'

Holmes nodded agreement. 'And the

tradesman ensures good marriages for his children with money in mind, which leaves only the lover and his lass, the only real romantics.

''Pon my word, what a cynical pair we are, Watson.' We puffed our pipes in silence for a while.

'I consider Jack the lad a possibility because he may have used his skill of walking on stilts to stride over the barriers, but then the theory collapses because we again come up against the confounded geese.' Both of us watched the bats flittering about, enjoying the peace and transient moments.

'Do you think, Holmes, in his roaming the world as a seaman and lastly his contacts with animal trainers in the circus, he might have learned some way of . . . somehow . . . using a means of mass hypnosis on the geese?'

Holmes did not reply, puffing away, no doubt considering my theory for what it was worth. I continued.

'When I was out in India the fakirs performed some feats one would hardly have thought possible. The eastern people seem to have a way with animals. I remember the snake-charmer's movement from side to side of his flute hypnotising the snake; the music is incidental and only for the benefit of the audience. We were told that snakes are deaf, I don't know how true this is. The point is, Holmes, could our Jack the lad have learnt some eastern magic or formula to soothe or calm the geese in some way?'

Holmes knocked the dottle from his pipe. 'Possibly, Watson, possibly, but I think unlikely; but it is an option we must keep open. Jack the lad, at the behest of her Ladyship, is a most likely suspect to carry out such a daring and spirited enterprise.'

Holmes chuckled. 'All this theorising on the assumption of an arrangement between Jack the lad and her Ladyship. Really, Watson, we should be ashamed.'

We walked out of the garden leaving the perfume of the roses to mingle with the aroma of pipe smoke and the little active hunters of the air. As we opened the huge main door of the Hall, a footman rose from his chair and, after taking our hats, began shooting the bolts to secure the place. Suddenly Holmes stopped, a look of renewed interest crossed his face and within seconds he had become galvanised into action.

'Go ahead, Watson, there is something I must do. I remember now the old viscount had a great interest in zoology . . . many of the shelves I noticed are devoted to the subject . . . suddenly I have had an idea. Good night, Watson, sleep well.' Without more ado, he rushed into the library telling the footman not to wait up for him as he might be some time.

I trod the curved stairway wearily, the fresh air appeared to have had a soporific effect upon me. I slept like I had been pole-axed.

Next morning, Holmes in spite of his nocturnal studying, which, I might add, he never referred to, was up before me and was waiting in the breakfast-room. On the sideboard under silver tureens were devilled kidneys, liver, ham, eggs, fried bread, mushrooms and tomatoes. 'A most admirable selection,' I exclaimed.

'Quite so, quite so, a little of each I think, Watson.'

His Lordship joined us and, reverting back to our army mess days, we read our newspapers propped up against toast racks and cruet sets, ignoring the niceties of polite convention. Fully satisfied we rose from the table, his Lordship still immersed in studying yesterday's cricket scores. Leaving the breakfast-room we encountered her Ladyship. She smiled and we exchanged the usual pleasantries, so it was a complete surprise to me upon Holmes being asked by her Ladyship if he was any nearer to bringing the case to a successful conclusion, he replied,

'I hope so, your Ladyship. Very soon. Perhaps in the next twenty-four hours.'

He looked across to me and said, 'Yes, Watson, I lay awake last night listening to a vixen fox barking in the woods and suddenly it came to me . . . however, no more until I have tested my theory further.' Her Ladyship was impressed, I was speechless.

We both spent the rest of the morning

fishing and the afternoon walking around the countryside.

Not once did Holmes refer to the disclosure he had made to her Ladyship earlier that morning, and I knew better than to ask for enlightenment.

After our evening meal of rabbit, veal and mushroom pie, followed by an excellent steamed pudding, all washed down with a fine bottle of wine from his Lordship's extensive wine cellar, Holmes put on his cape and deer stalker saying he had some business to attend to . . . I asked no questions as he slipped out into the night.

When he returned a couple of hours later, and I was on the point of retiring to bed, I asked him if all was well.

'All is very well, Watson, very well indeed. In fact, if all goes to plan we shall be away by the noon train tomorrow.'

I did not ask him for further details. Past experience of my friend had taught me that all would be revealed in the fullness of time.

Next morning her Ladyship entered the breakfast-room later than us. We had just finished and were about to rise and leave.

'Now, Mr Holmes, it is twenty-four hours since I asked you about the case. Then you replied that you may have news within the next twenty-four. Well, have you?'

Holmes rose from the table and half bowed. 'Yes, your Ladyship, I have news. In fact I was on the point of asking his Lordship if he would care to accompany Dr Watson and myself to the trophy house, to inspect the return of the trophies.'

The look upon all our faces was one of the utmost surprise and astonishment. His Lordship put down the paper he had been reading and looked up at Holmes with a completely blank face. 'Do you mean you have recovered the trophies . . . all three of them?'

'Yes, your Lordship, all three. They are back, hanging on the wall again.'

His Lordship stood up, the crumbs falling from his napkin. He placed the paper on the table and appeared unable to comprehend the situation. At last he said, 'But have you been to the trophy room then this morning . . . ?'

'No,' replied Holmes, 'but I have high hopes that when we do visit the trophy room, they will all be back in their respective places upon the walls.'

His Lordship looked across at her Ladyship who was still speechless and then back again to Holmes. 'Shall we go and see?' said Holmes taking the initiative.

'By all means,' replied his Lordship, still protesting his amazement at Holmes's disclosure.

He obtained the key from the safe in his study and soon we were all striding out towards the trophy house. All three of us took extra care stepping over the trip-wires and man-traps and presently stood together around the doorstep. The huge key was produced by his Lordship to open the door, but it was not needed; the door was closed but unlocked. He turned the handle and the heavy oak door swung back to reveal, upon examination, the three shields back again hanging on the walls.

His Lordship took them down each in turn and examined them and, except for a blade of grass wedged between the wood and the silver presentation plate on one of them, they were in perfect condition. He turned, as I did also to Holmes for an explanation, but before we uttered a word Holmes spoke.

'First, your Lordship, I must inform you that I cannot reveal the name of the thief.'

'You cannot reveal the name of the thief?' repeated the astonished peer. 'But why not, Holmes . . . after all, that is why I asked for your help in the first instance.'

'No, no,' said Holmes raising his hand in protest. 'I never promised to name the thief, only to try and solve the crime . . . I can assure your Lordship that there will never be a similar occurrence. In fact, I suggest that you get rid of all those man-traps, wires, shotguns . . . everything. There is bound to be an accident some time in the future, either to yourself or some member of your staff.'

'But I don't understand, Mr Holmes.

How can you promise me that my trophies will be safe in future?'

Holmes retorted, 'I can promise, your Lordship, because I have spoken with the thief. Now he knows that I know him, he cannot possibly take anything again, or I should reveal all.'

His Lordship was still baffled by Holmes's reluctance to reveal all. 'I still cannot understand why you will not reveal his name to me.'

'Because I have promised not to. It was part of the bargain I struck with him. Now if your Lordship will forget all about the burglaries and perhaps turn your energies to the running of the estate, I am sure you will have no more trouble.'

His Lordship sank down into one of the leather chairs and pulled his coat around him because it was chill, and no fire had been lit.

'I suppose you are right, Mr Holmes. I have spent far too much time and money on this trophy room. I know I have neglected the estate. Wilson, the estate manager, has been on to me for some time to give my consent to certain things that want doing.'

Holmes remarked, 'I'm sure it will please him.'

He turned suddenly to Holmes, 'Good heavens, it wasn't Wilson, was it?'

Holmes laughed and shook his head. 'No, no, on that you can be assured . . . is it agreed then, your Lordship; no more neglect of the estate in return for a promise that the trophies will be safe in the future?'

His Lordship raised his huge bulk from the chair and gave a wan smile. 'I suppose I must agree, Mr Holmes, but I should dearly like to know how the man managed to pull off such a daring theft. I do admire his skill and, yes, bravery . . . I don't suppose you would reveal how it was achieved . . . ?'

Holmes shook his head and said, 'I can assure you, your Lordship, he will never, ever, see you again . . . One last word, I should look to some of the repairs needed to the cottages on the estate first. I noticed, as I walked around the village and farm cottages,

271

tiles off roofs, broken chimney pots, rotting thatch . . . contented workers go a long way to make an estate a good estate . . . the locals still admire and speak with great respect of your father . . . this is an accolade we would all wish for, from those we leave behind.' Only Holmes could have pointed out to the good, but misguided, young viscount, the right path to take.

His Lordship accompanied us in his coach to the railway station and thanked us both for all we had achieved. I had done nothing to help solve the mystery, but good manners dictated I should be included in his gratitude. I felt the village people had, in the future, the kind of squire they deserved. We waved goodbye, and soon we were sat back watching the countryside slip by as we made our way back to London.

Holmes settled himself down and read the morning paper he had bought at the station bookstall, whilst I was content to read the book on carp fishing which his Lordship, knowing my interest in the sport, had generously given me. I was eager to learn the rest of the story: how Holmes had solved the mystery, the identity of the unnamed thief and, even more interesting, how the theft had been carried out.

Unfortunately, the carriage compartment was also occupied by a gentleman who was obviously going fishing by the amount of rods and tackle he had with him. I had to contain my curiosity and be satisfied to read how the monks had made artificial ponds in which to breed carp. Carp, once caught, would be wrapped in wet moss and kept alive until ready to be cooked.

I noticed our fisherman friend eyeing the cover of my book, and when the train began to slow down at the next station, he collected his tackle, saying as he alighted, 'I hope you enjoy reading your book as much as I hope to enjoy catching a nice fat carp.' I thanked him, and soon the train was moving again.

I looked at Holmes. He knew I was most anxious to hear the details, so, folding his newspaper and putting it aside, he began to relate the solving of the trophy house thefts. But only after a further delay whilst he charged his favourite meerschaum and made sure it was truly lit.

'Not, my dear Watson, biographer extraordinaire, I mentioned earlier that I felt the thief was perhaps an acquaintance of his Lordship, this was my reason for speaking to the butler. He was most helpful and provided me with a list of visitors who were from some of our most illustrious families. However, I never needed that list; I was wrong in thinking in that direction.' He dug a hand deep into his cape pocket and stretched his legs out. 'As I told his Lordship the other day when we first inspected the trophy house, an ordinary thief would hardly have bothered risking life and limb to obtain just one trophy. The value when melted down would have been very little, compared with the value he would have got by robbing the far less difficult Hall; taking small paintings and silver, easily disposed of to any antique dealer.'

Holmes looked at me in a rather quizzical way. 'It was when we were talking to the head gardener the other evening that first set me on the solution. It didn't strike me at the time; only the other night when I lay awake, listening to the far-away call of that vixen fox. I would point out that listening to the fox is totally unconnected with what I am about to disclose, but often our thoughts are like that, without rhyme or reason. Do you remember how, when we were discussing the garden exhibits with the head gardener, he made a remark about old Jim Roberts. He said something like . . . 'When t'others finish in the evening 'cause it's getting dark, old Jim just carries on. 'Tis all the same to 'im.'

'It came to me then, the one man who could negotiate that barrier of traps, wires and guns in the dark, would be old blind Jim. He often worked on the traps and guns during the day, helping his Lordship and the others. Blind people are often far more able to do difficult things than we who are blessed with sight. As you are well aware, Watson, the loss of their sight increases the sensitivity of their other senses.'

He paused a moment to catch a fleeting view of something by the trackside, then returned to his explanation. 'Old blind Jim could cross the barrier in the dark as well as in the daylight. It made not the slightest difference to him, his world was one of continuous darkness.'

I interrupted at this point, 'But what about the geese?'

'Ah! The geese, Watson . . . the geese. I thought you might ask about them. Geese only react to sounds or disturbances they are not used to. Old blind Jim used to whistle softly during the daytime when about his work, and the geese recognised that soft whistle in the dark . . . hence they were put at their ease and continued to be quiet.'

I agreed, seeing the logic of his reasoning.

Holmes continued, 'Once across the barrier he waited on the doorstep until the clock in the stable building chimed.' I looked at Holmes with what must have been a quizzical expression. He went on to explain.

'Sounds, as you are aware from your

old days in the army, travel many hundreds of yards at night . . . even small sounds. The click of the duplicate key he had copied, turning in the lock, might have been heard by any keeper nearby, so he timed the turning of the key to correspond with one of the chimes of the clock. Once inside he took a trophy from the wall, then left, closing the door behind him, having no need to lock it, of course. He returned as he came, across the barrier and back home.' Holmes reached out to prevent his newspaper from slipping onto the floor.

I took the opportunity to ask a question which puzzled me. 'But why did he do it? He had served with distinction in the army and his Lordship's father had employed him, when many like him would have ended begging on the streets . . . so why had he turned burglar?'

'I asked him the same question, Watson, the evening I slipped out and visited him in his cottage. I think I had already formed an opinion before I asked it. The night was cold, the fire was low, the room filled with smoke. It appeared the chimney was partly blocked. It wasn't a very comfortable place to live in, I can tell you; cold, wet and damp. His poor wife sat with blankets around her to keep warm. I heard her cough as I went up the path to the cottage; she hardly stopped coughing the whole time I was in the place. When I went up the stairs to the bedroom, at the request of old Jim, I saw large patches of wet on the floor where the rain came through the dislodged tiles. The dripping water from the ceiling fell on the bed and floorboards. Bowls and tins had been placed to catch the drips.'

I sympathised aloud to Holmes with the old couple's predicament.

Holmes went on. 'Old blind Jim felt it was a grave injustice that so much time and money should be spent on the silly trophy house, whilst his servants in the cottages had to put up with such terrible living conditions. Under his Lordship's father, things had been much better. The cottages had always been kept in good repair and the estate better managed, but his Lordship had been too interested in his trophy house to bother with managing things properly.'

Holmes opened up his cape, I did likewise with my coat; it had turned very warm in the carriage. 'You see, old Jim hoped that by taking a trophy, it would make his Lordship see how silly were his traps and things. When his plan did not work out he took another trophy. Afterwards, instead of scrapping the traps and guns, his Lordship actually spent more time and money on security.

'Jim did not know what to do next but, without coming up with any new idea, he decided to try once more. After the third theft we, of course, were called upon.'

I asked about the trophies. 'Oh! They were kept in Jim's attic. Every now and again he would bring them down to clean. He never meant of course to keep them. Some day he intended to return them. As honest as they come is old Jim Roberts.'

The train halted at a station and for a moment I thought our discussion would be interrupted as a very stout gentleman and a rather thin lady paused outside the carriage door, wondering whether to enter or not. However, the lady pulled on the arm of her companion and they walked further down the platform to secure an unoccupied compartment.

As the train drew out with steam and smoke drifting past the windows, Holmes continued his account. 'I made a promise to old Jim that I would not disclose his name, or how the theft had been committed, provided he returned the trophies that night. Also, I promised to do what I could to make his Lordship aware of his responsibility to the estate and his servants who relied upon him.'

Holmes once again eased his long frame from one position to another. I did the same. Somehow, we both seemed to find the journey beginning to get very tiresome indeed.

Holmes took up the story once again. 'I arranged that if he managed to return the trophies during the night, and all went well, he was to place a single goose feather between the door of the trophy house and the jamb, as a signal when I looked out of the library window next morning.'

I interrupted, 'You must have remarkably good eyesight, Holmes, to see a single feather at that distance.'

'Yes, I have good eyesight, but even I could not have seen it without the aid of the brass telescope his Lordship keeps on its tripod by a window of the library. Did you not notice it?'

I confessed I had not. 'So, that was how you were able to say, with such certainty, the trophies were back in the trophy house again.'

Holmes smiled, 'Exactly, my dear Watson.'

I continued, 'And when you said to his Lordship that the thief would not set eyes upon him ever again, you were speaking the truth. Poor blind Jim will never set eyes upon his Lordship or anyone ever again.'

'Yes,' said Holmes. 'I wanted his Lordship to think the crime had been committed by a common thief from outside the district. It would not have gone down well with him, I am sure, if he thought someone, a friend or a servant on the estate, had outwitted him and was inwardly laughing every time he saw his Lordship.'

How simple it all seemed when explained by Holmes, yet how baffling had it all seemed only twenty-four hours ago.

The train began to snake and slow down as it approached the outer network of track leading into the station. There was a squealing from the carriage wheels as they protested when taking some of the sharp curves.

'Now there's a puzzle for you to solve, Watson.'

'Puzzle . . . where?' I looked about me.

'Under your feet.'

I looked at the floor. 'You have the better of me, Holmes.'

The train came to a halt as it stood by a signal, awaiting the track ahead to clear.

Holmes replied, 'On a straight piece of rail track the wheels on each side of the axle revolve at the same speed, the revolutions equal. However, when the track curves, one wheel has to revolve faster than the other.'

I must have looked a little blank so Holmes decided to elucidate.

'Think of a boy and his train set. He sets up the track in a circle. Now, the outer rail of the circle is larger than the inner rail of the circle . . . correct?'

I agreed, but perplexed as to what it was all leading up to.

'So,' continued Holmes, 'the wheels on the outside rail then have to revolve faster than the wheels on the inside rail because there is more rail to traverse.'

I agreed again, but could still not comprehend where the puzzle was, and said so.

'I don't see any puzzle, Holmes. The wheels on the axle, just like those on a cab or coach, revolve at different speeds to compensate for this.'

To emphasise the grasp of my understanding I continued, 'When a cab turns to the left, the left-hand-side wheel revolves more slowly. Likewise, when the cab turns to the right, the right-hand wheel revolves more slowly. They revolve independently of each other on the axle.'

'That is absolutely correct, Watson, only there is a problem . . . the wheels on all railway rolling stock are fixed to the axle; rigid, solid, welded together. One wheel cannot revolve faster or slower than its partner on the same axle.

'When running on a straight piece of track, there is no problem, each wheel turning at the same revolutions as the other. The problem arises when the track begins to curve; whether to the left or right, the problem remains the same.

'As we see with the train set, the wheel on the outer rail has to revolve faster than the one on the inner rail . . . it's the law of physics . . . so how does rolling-stock cope with this problem when negotiating a curve, without twisting and wrecking the axle?'

I gave him a long look, not realising until then that railway rolling-stock did have their wheel fixed rigid to the axle. Any further thoughts on the subject were interrupted by the train jerking and beginning to move forward again. The familiar sound of clickety clack, clickety clack was heard as the wheels passed over points and crossovers, before the train glided to a halt inside the station.

Doors were flung open, porters dashed forward with wheelbarrows to assist with luggage; the whole familiar bustle and noise, so very different from the staid quiet country station we had entrained from. We waited in turn to give up our tickets and then were swept along again with the outpouring mass of humanity, like us, eager to leave the station.

Observing the demand for cabs, Holmes suggested we walk back to Baker Street as it would be just the thing to bring back the circulation to our legs, after our enforced inactivity.

We walked along the pavement by the side of a row of cabbies. The drivers struggling to assist the passengers enter their cabs, others were heaving and tugging at heavy luggage, intent upon securing it onto the roof-racks. Trade was roaring. As one cab left the rank and left a space, another filled it, the horse knowing exactly what was expected of it from years of experience.

I describe this scene because one particular cab was turning round as it was facing the wrong direction it was to go. We paused and watched the wheel nearest the pavement revolve several times, whilst the other one made perhaps half a turn as the cab completed its one hundred and eighty degree turn.

It was a perfect demonstration of the physical science of free-turning wheels on the same axle and, likewise, it revealed the problem involved with railway rolling stock; the wheels being fixed and unable to turn independently of each other created, so it would appear, enormous stresses on the wheels and axles, even when traversing the slightest curve.

We walked on, my brows knitted in deep thought. Obviously the problem, puzzle, call it what you may, had been solved long ago by pioneering railway engineers, yet it is never given a moment's thought by those who travel daily on the train. It was a first-class conundrum indeed.

I had the feeling that Holmes had a trace of a smirk on his face; however, I was determined to discover for myself the puzzle of the fixed railway wheels . . . but it would have to be all in good time. I have not the best mind when it comes to scientific matters.

We turned into Baker Street to be met with the familiar sights; street hawkers, flower sellers, newspaper boys shouting the latest headlines, all rubbing shoulders with the home-going workers.

Perhaps the countryside was quieter, but I was glad to be back and part of the London scene. I am sure Holmes was too, but sentiment was not one of his strongest points.

I closed the street door behind us and followed Holmes along the passageway and up the stairs to our rooms, but my mind was already back to trying to

solve the railway wheel puzzle. Could it
. . . no, no, perhaps not . . . but how
about . . . not that either . . . ? Holmes
had certainly set off a hare for me to
chase.